The K.A.T.H.I.N.S.
Project

By

Patrick Shackelford

Patrick Shackelford

The K.A.T.H.I.N.S. Project

Published by Patrick Shackelford at Smashwords

Library of Congress Catalog Number: 2017903497
ISBN: 978-0-692-85588-1

Acknowledgments

I would like to thank God, Baby P, Jessie, J, Nichole, Tae, Heather, Acosta, Connie, Joel, Paris, Irene, Roland Williams, Camp Joseph Scott, Dago, Papi Lap, PIZ-NAK, ROCKET, P2 GOOD and YOUNG OCTANE THE CATHOLIC.

Epilogue

The saying goes, many are called, but few are chosen. Nineteen Eighty-Six was a special year for the world. Mike Tyson won his first heavyweight championship fight, making him the youngest heavyweight to do so at the time. It was also the year; the United Nations had deemed to be the "International Year of Peace." The cold war was finally coming to an end, but this was partially due to the terrible Chernobyl disaster in Russia. However, there must have been some deeper, more esoteric knowledge to that decree because that was the year that each member of the K.A.T.H.I.N.S. project came into existence.

The K.A.T.H.I.N.S. (Kids at the Heart in Normal Society) were born under extraordinary circumstances. Whether if it was to parents of extreme wealth or intelligence, each one of these children's lives were dedicated to protecting the world. And we have monitored them from childhood to adulthood, watching them hone each of their special skills sets to make the world a better place. We've also been monitoring the other side too. He knew of these special beings and have travelled many galaxies to stop them. He has also been studying and waiting.

It is now 2016 and the K.A.T.H.I.N.S. have all grown into young adults. They have reached the age of maturity when all of the young prophets of old began to show the world their true purpose on earth. Each prophet spoke of the one who would follow in line. The ones who would move forward with the "Ultimate Plan." Some of the prophets of yesteryear were meant to prepare, others were meant to minister, but these six individuals were meant to save the world. Their day jobs helped the less fortunate; but their true calling was to stop the evil forces of Amdogata, an evil, otherworldly spirit who can take on the form of innocent people and machines.

Children are his life force. Amdogata feeds off of their pure energy, innocence and unconditional love. He sates himself by corrupting children. The K.A.T.H.I.N.S. protect the kids from this evil while maintaining a normal, everyday working environment and identity. Their normal human identities also protect them from being discovered. In order to completely destroy the world as well as the guardians, Amdogata has been trying to gain access to the only weapon strong enough to do so, the Secret Scrolls.

The Secret Scrolls with their ancient teachings and magick hold all of the galaxies' truths. The original Scrolls are buried in strategic places all over the world, deep in the earth's crust. Only those known as the Powers That Be know where they are. However, they remain untouched in the Latter World where only special individuals can come to praise and speak with the Gods of Yore. The Latter World is where the K.A.T.H.I.N.S. received their training and understanding of the teachings the Secret Scrolls possessed.

The true guardians of our realm, the Powers That Be along, with our help, have provided protection to these six individuals as they grew up. Under the guidance of The Powers That Be, we have provided them with special vehicles and suits, which were made with special material from The Latter World, all that assists the K.A.T.H.I.N.S. in protecting the realm. Now as Amdogata's forces became stronger and headed towards Earth, it was time to let them fly. To let them go forward with the "Ultimate Plan."

.

Moral Message of the Scrolls.

Don't be afraid to ask for help.
Help is all around you.

THE
K.A.T.H.I.N.S.
PROFILES

Classified Top Secret

YOUNG OCTANE THE K.A.T.H.I.N.S.
A.K.A
PATRICK SHACKELFORD

HEIGHT: 6'2.

WEIGHT: 185.

ETHNIC BACKGROUND: Unknown.

K.A.T.H.I.N.S. SUIT: Black. When working, tie and slacks.

VEHICLES: High Octane.

FAMOUS QUOTE: "Just that real just that pure".

JOB: Lead Aid Programmer at Western Avenue Elementary School.

RESIDENCE: Grace Street in Inglewood California with mom and Altadena California with his father on Woodbury.

K.A.T.H.I.N.S. CONTRIBUTIONS: Leader of the KAT.H.I.N.S. Interpreter of the Secret Scrolls and talks to The Powers That Be.

EXTRA CURRICULAR ACTIVITIES: Attends Dominguez University at night and visits his grandmother in the morning before work.

MODERN DAY
A.K.A
MALIK CONWAY

HEIGHT: 5'8.

WEIGHT: 150.

ETHNIC BACKGROUND: African-American.

K.A.T.H.I.N.S SUIT: Blue. When working, street clothes.

VEHICLES: Copilot of High Octane.

FAMOUS QUOTE: "My assumptions as we"".

JOB: Barber at Nice Nelsons Salon.

RESIDENCE: 80th and Van ness in Los Angeles California. Malik lives with his father and mother. His father studies the history on The Powers That Be.

K.A.T.H.I.N.S CONTRIBUTIONS: Has meaningful dreams that help lead the K.A.T.H.I.N.S. to the Secret Scrolls.

EXTRA CURRICULAR ACTIVITIES:
Attends USC at night and loves to use public transportation.

VEHICLE

HIGH OCTANE

K.A.T.H.I.N.S. Mode: Two laser machine guns come out the side doors. Turbo pipes come from the bottom of the trunk. Missile launcher on the top of the hood. Has a force field. Nitro's turn the car red in KAT.H.I.N.S. form. Inside the vehicle an extra monitor comes up from the floor and a Joystick comes from the passenger seat to control weapons. Car also rises 4 inches off the ground. A stick shift comes from the right armrest to give High Octane four extra gears.

Top Speed: 200mph.

K.A.T.H.I.N.S. Mode: 1700 mph.

Color: Yellow under clear titanium.

K.A.T.H.I.N.S. Mode: Red, due to nitro fluid running through the clear titanium.

Ability: Turbo boosts 55 feet off the ground into the air. Also, has 5 second countdown to turbo thrust.

Downfall: Turbo boost and turbo thrust can't be used simultaneously, only two minutes apart.

Driver: YOUNG OCTANE THE
K.A.T.H.I.N.S

MAVERICK
A.K.A
CHAD

HEIGHT: 6'1.

WEIGHT: 183.

ETHNIC BACKGROUND: Caucasian.

K.A.T.H.I.N.S. SUIT: Red. When working, blue jeans and tee shirt.

VEHICLES: Sky Guardian.

FAMOUS QUOTE: "Yes, yes exactly".

JOB: Mechanical Engineer

RESIDENCE: Pasadena Hills.

K.A.T.H.I.N.S. CONTRIBUTIONS: Works on all the high-powered vehicles for The K.A.T.H.I.N.S.

EXTRA CURRICULAR ACTIVITIES: Helps those with special needs

VEHICLE

SKY GUARDIAN TURBO CHARGED HAWK HELICOPTER

K.A.T.H.I.N.S. Mode: At all times. Multiple Laser cannons come out of the side wings. Missile launchers and plasma cannons come from under the wings. Has a Force Field. The inside has 6 seats and monitors in each headrest.

K.A.T.H.I.N.S. Speed: Light speed.

Color: Teal green under clear titanium.

Ability: Flies like a jet and helicopter.

Downfall: Cannot fly in space.

Home: Pasadena California.

Pilot: Maverick

THE DIPLOMAT
A.K.A
DARREL

HEIGHT: 5'10.

WEIGHT: 199

ETHNIC BACKGROUND: African-American.

K.A.T.H.I.N.S. SUIT: Grey. When working, business suits.

VEHICLES: Karma.

FAMOUS QUOTE: "We are not here for ourselves; we are here for the people".

JOB: Public Relations Manager for The K.A.T.H.I.N.S.

RESIDENCE: Mansion in La Vina, California. The Diplomat's house is also the K.A.T.H.I.N.S. Headquarters.

K.A.T.H.I.N.S. CONTRIBUTIONS: Keeps The KAT.H.I.N.S. out of trouble with the FBI.

EXTRA CURRICULAR ACTIVITIES:
Darrel likes to visit his father's grave after every mission.

VEHICLE

KARMA

K.A.T.H.I.N.S. Mode: Two laser machineguns come out of the side doors. Turbo pipes drop from the bottom of the truck. Missile launcher comes from the top of the hood with a force field. Inside the vehicle an extra monitor comes from the floor and a Joystick comes out from the passenger seat to control weapons. Truck rises six inches from the ground.

Top Speed: 130 mph.

K.A.T.H.I.N.S. Mode: 850 mph.

Color: Black under clear titanium.

K.A.T.H.I.N.S. Mode: Blue, due to nitro fluid running through the clear titanium.

Ability: Turbo boosts 50 feet off the ground into the air. Has 8-second countdown to turbo thrust.

Downfall: Turbo boost has to be cleared by the K.AT.H.I.N.S. Headquarters.

Driver: THE DIPLOMAT.

MARIA
A.K.A
THE MERCIFUL

HEIGHT: 5'3.

WEIGHT: 121

ETHNIC BACKGROUND: Hispanic.

K.A.T.H.I.N.S. SUIT: Violet. When working, street clothes.

VEHICLES: SD1.

FAMOUS QUOTE: "Simply Marvelous".

JOB: Downtown Homeless Shelter.

RESIDENCE: Eastside of Los Angeles.

K.A.T.H.I.N.S. CONTRIBUTIONS: Houses the Secret Scrolls.

EXTRA CURRICULAR ACTIVITIES: Dancing and singing.

VEHICLE

SD1 (SUPER DYNAMIC) TURBO CHARGED KAWASAKI MOTORCYCLE

K.A.T.H.I.N.S. Mode: Two lasers come from two extra exhaust pipes on the side of SD1. Missile launcher shoots from front headlight. Has turbo thrust from Booster in the back booster. SD1 also has a force field.

Top Speed: 150mph.

K.A.T.H.I.N.S. Mode: 1000 mph.

Color: Red under clear titanium.

K.A.T.H.I.N.S. Mode: Black due to nitro fluid.

Ability: Countdown is five seconds. Can turbo boost 70 feet of the ground, while going 1000 mph.

Downfall: Little protection.

Driver: THE MERCIFUL.

ALKALINE
A.K.A
APRIL

HEIGHT: 5'7.

WEIGHT: 135

ETHNIC BACKGROUND: Caucasian.

K.A.T.H.I.N.S. SUIT: Turquoise. When working, business suit.

VEHICLES: Space Hawk.

FAMOUS QUOTE: "If you want to talk about right, then you want to talk about wrong".

JOB: Assistant Public Relations Manager for the K.A.T.H.I.N.S.

RESIDENCE: Mansion overlooking the Pacific Ocean in Palos Verdes, California.

K.A.T.H.I.N.S. CONTRIBUTIONS: Assists the Diplomat in writing media content. Her father and The Diplomat's father were best friends. The two old friends created the K.A.T.H.I.N.S. vehicles before being killed by Amdogata.

EXTRA CURRICULAR ACTIVITIES:
Provides public relations for companies and
donates money to charity funds on behalf of
The K.A.T.H.I.N.S.

VEHICLE

SPACE HAWK TURBO-CHARGED
PHANTOM AIRPLANE

K.A.T.H.I.N.S. Mode: At all times. Space Hawk has eight plasma ray cannons and four missile launchers on its flexible wings. Left wing has a vessel for High Octane to be stored for space missions. Right wing has a vessel for Karma. Top middle has a vessel for SD1, and underneath Space Hawk, has a vessel for Sky Guardian. Space Hawk also has a force field.

K.A.T.H.I.N.S. Speed: Super light speed.

Color: Silver under pure titanium.

Ability: No Flaws, perfect

Home: Under the Palos Verdes' Mountains. Comes out from the sea.

Pilot: ALKALINE

1

It is always night on Planet Limbo. Not one star in the sky; instead, gray-colored clouds that were set afire with blue lightning, decorated the sky. It was the only light that illuminated the planet and that was the way it should be. With each flash of blue lightning, one could see the agony and pain of the inhabitants of Planet Limbo. It was a place where one could never find rest. Their souls were sucked away from them, their spirits defeated; the heavy weight of corruption hunched their shoulders. They were slaves to their egos, to their iniquities, to the Ancient Evil One.

He was the all-seeing one, the destroyer of conscience. He was the overseer of all this, a being that was older than our concept of time. He was neither created nor born, he just appeared out of the abyss, fully formed, with a hunger for the destruction of innocence, of purity, of love.

His name was Amdogata.

The Ancient One.

The Evil One.

The One whose hunger was never sated.

He resided in Cave Cogneto, a dark cavern that was said to be filled with the souls of innocent children who later became the mad men and women of the world. The men and women who slaughtered millions because of prejudice and sport. He fed off all of them. However, over the billions of lives he claimed across the galaxies, his hunger could never be satisfied.

Amdogata sat there, arms folded, looking at his minions. He was furious and the skies reflected his anger. He was going to make them pay. Every single last one of them. As he had done with all societies and planets that came before. He had searched for the Scrolls for time infinitum and they have always eluded him. Each land, each galaxy he had found them in; the guardians of that realm would conceal them away. And each time he conquered, he would scorch the land underneath, where no being could ever reside.

Ashes to ashes and Earth would be no exception.

Amdogata stood and walked outside of his cavern and addressed his army underneath. As he approached, all ears and eyes were lifted, waiting for his commands. He spoke, a searing, deep voice, the very embodiment of hate.

"I have found the Scrolls. They have been found on Gaia, the third planet in the Milky Way Galaxy. I want all of you to go to earth and find them. There will be no excuses whatsoever."

Amdogata looked at the sky. It began to turn a dark red, reminiscent of the blood of his enemies. It was a sign of victory. He then looked down at his army again, his eyes filled with glee. He continued to speak,

"You are to find an earthling that can assist you in your objective. All you will tell them is that you work for Amdogata the Legislator of Limbo. Once they hear that, I will proceed from there."

The Serin were Amdogata's greatest weapon. He created them from the Elements, forged from metal, thunder and the ashes of fallen civilizations. Their coloring was the deep black-red of dried blood, their eyes the same color as bile. They were forged from suffering. Zemen, one of his most loyal commanders stepped to the cavern's edge. He kneeled to the ground and looked up at Amdogata.

"What should we look for in a subject? I mean ..."

Amdogata raised his hand, silencing Zemen.

"Silence!" Amdogata yelled, "You will know the subject by what you feel."

Zozetal the lesser was always eager to show his allegiance to Amdogata. He was ruthless on the battlefield. He never left a body behind, no matter if it was a man, woman or child. He also stepped forward and kneeled.

"What is ...?" Zozetal asked,

Amdogata interrupted, "I said, SILENCE! Whoever finds the subject first, will be greatly rewarded. Once they are found, you are all to head back to Limbo immediately. However, while you are on Gaia, you all will take on human form and will live like earthlings."

His army listened intently, eager to forge ahead. Amdogata continued,

"What that means my subjects is talk, sleep and work as if you are all actual human beings. Now, get in your vehicles and proceed to earth at once. As you look for the scrolls, leave no stone unturned."

Zemen stood. Grabbing his sword, he bellowed the battle cry of the Serin. It was followed by Zozetal. Soon all of Limbo echoed with the sounds of impending doom. They packed up their weapons and ran to their vehicles. Thousands of them masquerading as comets and asteroids as they made their way towards Earth.

Amdogata smiled.

"The scrolls shall be mine." He said.

2

Southern California was indeed a beautiful place. It had everything, beaches, mountains, valleys, deserts and everything in between. Decembers were glorious with eighty-degree days and sixty-degree nights. The only snow you saw was in the mountains or on the slopes at Big Bear or Mammoth Mountain. The only bad thing about California, Todd Gross thought, was the smog. The sun had already set at five pm. The night sky was pitch black but it didn't allow him to see the stars at night.

As he stood outside of Gross Industries, he was determined to figure out a way to see all of the stars at night.

"Something has to be done about this smog. I'll see what I can do."

Gross Industries was one of the premier aerospace and defense manufacturers in the world. Todd was third generation CEO of the company, who founded by his grandfather was instrumental in building airplane engines and jet turbines during World War 2. Todd always saw himself as being forward-thinking; his family was one of the first major companies to hire women and minorities, with them working side by side. He felt that made him more cosmopolitan, more inclusive, innovative. And he used that to his advantage.

Todd carried the family name into a multibillion-dollar industry, expanding into robotics that were used in entertainment and construction. He also dabbled in the arts as well. He was a millionaire by the time he was twenty-seven and a billionaire by the time he was forty. He wanted to save the earth, or at least that's what he thought he wanted to do, however, his methods of doing so were a little bit... unconventional.

He still stood there, staring at the sky.

"I won't be able to see the signs. The signs that tell me that it is time. Time to put everything together."

For the past three months, Todd had been having dreams, chaotic dreams, visions of black metal and red skies, blue lightning and glowing, jaundiced eyes. The dreams didn't scare him. They intrigued him. And they became more vivid as time went on. Todd felt he was chosen by something. Something that was bigger than him.

Frankly, he needed this. He had all the earthly pleasures, it was time for him to do something greater than he ever thought he could. Whatever it was, he was at their command. So, he listened and waited for the sign. It was getting close to the winter solstice and he knew the dreams were correlated with that. He looked up again and saw all he needed to see. What he was waiting for. He knew it was now the time.

Beautiful streaks of gold dotted across the sky, as if it was a meteor shower. People stopped and stared. Cars almost ran into each other. Everyone was trying to get a glimpse of this phenomenon. Todd smiled and looked down at his phone. It was pinging. News stories were trying to determine what it was. No one knew what it was. Not even NASA. But Todd knew. He always knew.

Todd ran back inside his building and took the elevator to his penthouse office. He ran over to his window, where his state of the art telescope pointed towards the moon. He spun it around so that he could follow the sparkling golden orbs; they all seemed to be gathering in the San Fernando Mountains. Yet, there was no crash or bright explosions.

Nothing.

He counted at least fifty, but there had to be at least a hundred more that entered the earth's atmosphere. His phone started ringing off the hook. He already calculated at least another one hundred million being added to the company's coffers. However, that was not his priority right now. He was interested in where these orbs landed, all of them seemingly in the same spot. This was not an attack, at least not yet. He would have to go and investigate one day. Then the sky went dark.

It had begun.

The story passed within two days. There were a couple conspiracy theorists who rattled off about the Anunnaki, alien invasions or a government attacks on California. Even rumors of John Titor were being tossed about, however Todd paid them no mind. He just knew. It took him a week to pinpoint the area where they landed. Using his GPS, he hiked to the spot to find... absolutely nothing. Not a trace of anything. No metals, no scorch marks. Nothing.

He pulled out his Geiger counter. No radioactivity. Todd looked around him and screamed. The birds, scared from the sudden intrusion into their home, fled from their trees. Todd cracked his neck to the side and hiked back to his car. He knew this wasn't the last time he would see something like this. He would just have to wait and see.

****

They came. They landed. They assimilated. It has been two months since the golden dance in the sky and the humans were none the wiser. They emerged from their orbs, their vessels molding into human form. Two months passed, and the Serin were working and living all over the Valley.

They were disguised as men, women and children and their sole goal was to assimilate and destroy from within. At first glance, one wouldn't notice that anything was wrong with them, however, upon further inspection, you would notice a strange, dim glow in their pupils. Something not human, and that would be the last thing the poor soul saw before being sucked into the abyss.

In their spare time, they searched for the one Amdogata said would be the catalyst, the connection between the two worlds. For the past two months, they had no such luck. Zozetal, now known as Matt and Zemin who took on the name, David were afraid of returning empty-handed. They knew Amdogata would have their heads. They finally found their luck in February.

A young man was standing outside of his office complex as his dog sniffed around, looking for a place to relieve itself. Zozetal walked up and stood in front of Todd.

"Hello Todd."

Todd met his gaze and smirked. "Who are you? Better yet, who do you think you're talking to, young man?"

Zozetal smirked and widened his eyes. He was prepared to remove the soul from this pitiful, arrogant human being right where he stood. However, something about this man, stopped him. His pupils glowed, like theirs.

"That's not important, but what is important is that I am a regent for Amdogata, Prince of Limbo!"

Something came over Todd. His pupils glowed a golden-red and his facial expression changed. He looked like a mad man. Like a Serin.

"Say no more." He replied. "I'll show you where to go."

Zozetal followed Todd into his building. They took an elevator that led to the lower level of the building. They walked up to a metal door with a small pad located next to it. Todd put his hand on the pad, which read his palm print. The doors opened to a hallway. Making a right, a left and another right, the two men walked in. Zozetal smiled. Todd turned to him.

"You think this will be sufficient?" Todd asked.

Zozetal walked around it and turned to Todd. "Amdogata will be most pleased."

3

Every time his alarm rang, the famous verse by Ice Cube would permeate the air. "Just waking up in the morning, gotta thank God…

Patrick, known as Young Octane to a treasured few, would bolt out of his bed and get his day started. It was always the same routine. He would run to the bathroom, shower, brush his teeth and wash his face. He would quickly get dressed and come downstairs as he always did to a breakfast that was prepared by his mom. Except this time, he owned the home and his mother, who was on dialysis, stayed with him.

"Doing these little things kept her sane," he reasoned. He just wanted to make her life a little more comfortable until she could find a kidney. It broke his heart that he was unable to donate one of his own to her; however, she was still active and agile. She just had a little hiccup. It would all work out soon. He knew it would.

Patrick came downstairs to a plate of home-style potatoes, eggs and country fried steak with white gravy. "This would definitely hit the spot," he thought as he sat down.

"So, you get some good rest, mom?" Patrick asked as he stuffed his face.

"Yes. Better than most nights."

"I can see." He said.

"Don't stuff your mouth so full. You're going to choke."

Patrick swallowed and laughed. "You've been telling me this since I was a little kid."

"Some things never change." His mom said, smiling.

It felt good to see her smile. She had been through so much. With his dad passing away a couple years ago and her health problems, he was happy that he was there to be able to take care of her and be her rock.

His mom took a couple sips of her coffee as he finished eating. Once he was done, he put the plates in the sink and walked over to the front door. Patrick put on his jacket and grabbed his keys.

"Have a great day today. I'll call later." His mom smiled and waved. It was the best way to start his day. Patrick walked into the garage.

It was a good thing that his mother never went into the garage. He wouldn't know how to explain his vehicle to her. He normally drove her car when he was running errands with her. He didn't want her to think he was into the wrong things.

High Octane was laced. It was fly. It was flashy. It attracted female attention, and that was in its normal mode. When it was at full throttle, there was nothing you could tell him, the feeling was indescribable. He was going to drive incognito today. He was going to his normal place of employment. He drove the streets from Inglewood to Western Boulevard Elementary, where he worked as a lead air programmer. It was an easy drive but that's because he often left at six thirty in the morning. School didn't start until seven fifty.

Teaching was early days and late nights, but it was rewarding. He loved that he could shape future minds. Patrick always set up the lessons for the day by seven forty so that he could be outside to greet the kids. Today was no different. Standing near the principal, Patrick greeted each child with a high five. Two of his favorite students, Martin and Samantha walked up and greeted him at the gate.

Martin smiled and gave Patrick a hug. He exclaimed, "Mr. Shackifo, we love you."

Samantha, his twin sister chimed in, "Yes, Mr. Shackifo."

Patrick smiled, "Hey my little friends, I love you all as well." He said, "Now, who wants some candy?"

Before Samantha or Martin could answer, James, one of their classmate yelled as he walked in, "Me! Mr. Shackelford."

Patrick smiled, "Candy for all of you."

They smiled as they walked in. The warning bell rang. It was time to start the day.

4

There was nothing more beautiful to
Maria than Downtown Los Angeles. It was the
perfect mixture of grittiness, raw beauty and
angst that fed her soul. The yin and the yang,
the despair and happiness. The contradiction is
what fueled her work as a residential manager at
a homeless shelter. It also shaped her art as
well. Maria was a dancer and before dawn she
would often climb the stairs to the rooftop and
let the rising sun guide her movements. It was a
workout that not only worked her muscles but
also moved the spirit.

Maria came from a family of artists. She
grew up in the Pico-Union neighborhood of Los
Angeles, a small community that was a stone's
throw away from Downtown Los Angeles.
DTLA, as she affectionately called it, looked
way different than what it used to. When she
was growing up, it was mainly populated by
government officials by day and by the
homeless at night. Back then, the streets were
littered with needles and empty vials,
depression and mania. But it was beautiful
because it was real, it was organic.

Now, the element was still there, but it
was contained to one area, the infamous Skid

Row. It was surrounded by craft beer bars and vintage video game restaurants, organic grocery stores and luxury apartments. Downtown LA was in a revival and playground for the creative and the "well-off." At least those who appeared well-off on paper. When Maria would walk through DTLA, after passing through skid row, she often thought,

"Most of the people are just one paycheck away. I feel more for them, than the ones who owned their existence. The need to impress others was the main cause of all of this."

After she finished dancing, she showered, got dressed and made her way downstairs to serve breakfast to the residents. Her favorite resident, William, or Willie as he liked to be called, was up next in line. He winked at her and smiled.

"Hello Maria. How are you today?

"Just fine, Willie. Here, take some extra hash browns. They're good for you. How have you been? Maria asked.

Willie winked at Maria. "You're such a nice girl, but unfortunately I haven't been doing good at all. You see, my wife, Sueann, has come down with some type of fever. We don't have the money we need to get her medical attention. We're blessed we have this place to come to, but there's only so much that can be done."

Maria grabbed Willie's hand. "Oh no, you haven't been able to take her to emergency or urgent care.

Willie shook his head, "We don't have the time to wait. I'd rather just give her soup and bundle her up. If she gets any worse, then I will take her in."

"Oh Willie, I'm so sorry." Maria said with sympathy in her voice.

Willie pointed to the television screen that was mounted on the wall. He turned back to Maria with concern in his eyes. "Check out the news, darling. What in the tarnation?"

Maria squinted her eyes as she watched the TV screen. Her mouth dropped open as she watched the scene unfold.

5

The morning went by too fast. While teaching multiplication, Patrick looked up at the clock. It was nine thirty-two, two more minutes until the bell and recess. He stood up and walked to the front of the class.

"Alright, class, two more minutes before it's that time of the day. RECESS."

The kids cheered and started to get up from their desk. Patrick stopped them,

"You already know the drill. Before the bell rings, clean up your spaces and line up at the door. You now have two minutes."

Through a round of sighs, the children began to gather up their things and line up at the door by table number. Patrick walked up to the door and opened it, just as the bell rang.

"You're free." He said as the kids ran out the door, screaming. Patrick followed afterwards.

Patrick was always on morning recess duty. His part of the yard was where the second and third graders played. It was one of his favorite times of the day. The sun gave him the much-needed energy to power himself for the rest of the day. Being a program aid was easy, compared to what he did outside of work.

Serra was hanging upside down off of the jungle gym. She looked like she was going to try and flip off of the bar. Patrick blew his whistle and called out.

"Be careful, Serra. You're going to fall if you keep swinging around like that."

Serra nodded her head and lifted up, putting her hands on the bars and swung off of the jungle gym, landing on her feet.

"Just like cats." Patrick said to himself. Andy, one of his other students ran up and pulled on his shirt. Patrick looked down and smiled.

"Ooh, can I help you with the snacks Mr. Shackifo?"

Patrick smiled. He always thought it was hilarious the way kids pronounced his last name. He usually allowed them to call him Mr. Shackifo, Mr. Shack or Mr. S for short. They usually got it right by the end of the year.

"Yes, yes let's get the keys from Mr. Albertson."

As they walked over to Mr. Albertson's office, Patrick said to Andy, "Hey Andy."

Andy looked up at him. 'Yes, Mr. Shackifo."

"Always remember that, you are a special child. It's wonderful that you always want to help others."

Andy smiled. He then ran over to Mr. Albertson to get the keys. Patrick smiled as he watched him run away.

"Everything is perfect." Patrick said to himself.

6

Sometimes, the connection to the other worlds was too much for Alkaline. She prayed every night that it wouldn't drive her crazy where she wouldn't be effective to the world anymore. She hated being a diviner. It served its purpose in that she was able to see into the future, but the visions were stronger at night. And it kept her up. That was the reason why she took the night shift at the hospital where she volunteered. It allowed her to balance everything out.

But now it was four o'clock in the day and she felt and saw everything that Amdogata was planning. She knew she had to tell the others about what was going on. She felt like it might be too late. She tossed and turned. Her body was trying to wake up but she wouldn't allow herself too. Alkaline had to finish the dream. She had to prepare.

All she saw, was flashed of red, black and blue. She felt pain and the constant storms of suffering and despair. It was Amdogata. He knew the scrolls were here and had his sights set on Gaia. He called it the old name. He wanted to take over Earth. Amdogata was standing on top of a cliff. His cape, dyed blood red, flowed in the wind. His yellow eyes glowed. He stood outside his cave and spoke to Alkaline.

"I sense the Scrolls are on planet Earth. I must defeat The Powers That Be and the only way I can do that is to gather all of the Secret Scrolls. The Scrolls hide the key to all the wisdom of the universe. I must have that wisdom, without it, good will always prevail over evil and that cannot be. My only problem is the K.A.T.H.I.N.S.; I must get to the Scrolls before they do. And yes, I know you hear me, K.A.T.H.I.N.S. I want you to hear me because it's already too late."

Amdogata lifted his right hand in the air and started to shriek, a bloodcurdling cry. The atmosphere followed. Thunder and lightning streaked across the sky as the fires blew high in the air. The ash from the volcanoes fell to the ground. Amdogata continued,

"I will control The Latter World, K.A.T.H.I.N.S., and destroy The Powers That Be!"

Amdogata then walked back into his cave. Alkaline woke up in a sweat. It was five in the afternoon.

It has already begun.

7

"It has been two months of research and I still can't seem to find anything on what happened. It's so weird, but then again that is how the media is. Out of sight, out of mind. It used to be that a story took a couple of days to blow over, but now it's a couple of hours at the most. Scary..." Darrel thought to himself. He was hunched over his MacBook Pro in his mansion in Bel Air.

The San Fernando Valley was not too far from him, right off the 405 and 101, or if you took the roads, right on the other side of Topanga Canyon or Mulholland Road. The Diplomat, as he was affectionately called by his friends, was the mastermind behind the stories, or as he would call it, the deflection tactics of the K.A.T.H.I.N.S. Receiving his degree in journalism from USC as well as being a Rhodes scholar, certainly more than qualified him for the position of publicist to the group. His main job was to keep the K.A.T.H.I.N.S. out of trouble, which was a very difficult task.

As they got older, things seemed to be getting harder, not just in terms of everyday life, but with the various dangers the group faced. They all had jobs, hobbies and even went out on dates, but they had to juggle this with an increasing amount of activity that came from other realms. They all met when they were children and together, they've fought monsters and otherworldly beings within and around the earth's realm. They received much of their protection from the Powers that Be, but it was only so long before they would run across the government's radar. That was what he feared the most.

Even though, he knew they were fiction, he often compared the K.A.T.H.I.N.S. to the Avengers or X-Men, even Voltron. He saw how those groups were seen by the citizenry and government, and although, they were grateful for the help, humans tended to quickly turn their backs on those who saved them.

The Diplomat continued to research. He was cross-referencing stories from NASA, USGS and NOAA. None of them mentioned anything about the occurrence. Only stories he could find ranged from a light show to conspiracies about alien invasions and government attacks. It was so strange though. The orbs disappeared into an area near the Santa Monica and San Fernando Mountains without any sound or other evidence of impact. It was strange. And frightening.

Whenever something weird happened, which it inevitably would, the K.A.T.H.I.N.S. eventually became involved. Diplomat would be the first to know and come up with a game plan to make the problem go away as quickly as possible. This time, he felt that he wouldn't be so lucky.

"I don't want to be caught off-guard." He said to himself.

He had been waiting for Amdogata to make a move for a long time. Throughout the years of studying the scrolls, he knew that Amdogata would stop at nothing to get them and take over the galaxies. The K.A.T.H.I.N.S. have been successful in staving off the threat. He then heard a weird hum. It was low, guttural. It made his heart skip a beat. He turned towards his radio.

"What is going on? What is this strange signal?"

Darrel got up and walked towards his radio. The sound was getting stronger. It caused strange vibrations to flow through his body. All of a sudden, he saw a flash of lightning out of the corner of his eye.

"Amdogata must be behind this."

He ran back to his computer and prepared his attack.

8

"That Trade Tech education came in handy." Malik said as he was tinkering around with Sky Guardian downstairs in his basement.

"But that Northridge degree really put me over the top." He said with a smile. And that's one of the reasons why they called him the Maverick. He always did things differently. When he was in high school, he was into robotics and often participated in the competitions. Once he graduated, he went to Trade Tech to learn how to fix cars and finished with his degree in mechanical engineering from CSUN. He made sure to put his skills to good use.

He worked for Gross Industries, designing some of the latest technology. Although Gross Industries was known for its military defense, they also did other cool things like robotics. Maverick worked in the prosthesis department that specialized in androids and robotic limbs. He loved the fact that his creations helped people to become more mobile and live a better life. He also used those skills and technology to upgrade the K.A.T.H.I.N.S. vehicles.

Maverick always liked noise in the background. It was the one thing that always helped him focus on the task at hand. It was normally some type of music but today, he was listening to his TV. His secret hobby was watching The Chew. Maverick also liked to call himself a mechanic in the kitchen. The show was interrupted by a breaking news segment. Most of the time he didn't pay those any mind, but something that was said caught his interest. He turned his head to the TV and watched.

"Billionaires always buy themselves crazy things that we, mere mortals, can only dream of. However, this one takes the cake. Todd Gross, the CEO of Gross Industries has just bought three large swaths of land in the Santa Monica and San Fernando Mountains. He is also in negotiations to purchase two smaller robotics companies that focus on android production."

Maverick cocked his head to the side and continued to stare at the TV. The newscaster continued,

"Maybe he is trying to find a new building for Gross Industries or maybe he's finding a new site for a summer home. Either way, this is big. We'll give you more details at the twelve o'clock hour."

Maverick reached over to the table and turned off the TV. He walked back over to Sky Guardian and continued to tinker with the solar panels that powered the battery. He added some recent changes to the vehicle, ensuring that it ran on solar power and hydrogen when necessary. The only pollution it would leave behind would be water mist. When it was noon, Maverick went over to his phone and dialed.

9

The Diplomat was typing on his computer, trying to find any clue to see if Amdogata was involved in this recent celestial incident when he is suddenly interrupted by a phone call. Each K.A.T.H.I.N.S. had their own ringtone. The ringtone was "Classic Man" by Jidenna. He knew that it was Maverick. He stopped typing and put the phone to his ear.

"Hello?" He answered.

"Diplomat?" Maverick said, "Check out the news, good buddy!

Diplomat turned around and turned on his 70-inch smart TV.

"What channel, Mav?"

"Channel Seven."

Diplomat turned the TV to channel seven. The news had just started and Kelly Yamamoto was on the air. She was standing in front of Gross Industries.

"Hi, I'm Kelly Yamamoto for channel seven news. Earlier today, we informed you that multi-billionaire Todd Gross bought over three large pieces of land in the Santa Monica Mountains near San Fernando Valley. However, we have received updates that he has bought nearly thirty percent of all the privately-owned land in the San Fernando Valley. There is no indication as to what he is planning to do with this land, but witnesses say they have seen strange equipment moving into a location inside the mountains. It is a coincidence that he has bought land around this particular location."

Kelly ran up to a guard that was standing by an equipment truck.

"Sir, sir, can I talk to you? What is going on, what does ...?

The guard starts to point at the newscaster. "If you know what's good for you, lady; you'll get out of here right now." The guard put his hand over the camera lens.

"Get that camera out of my face!" He said.

"What do you mean?" Kelly asked.

The Diplomat noticed that the guard was trying his best to avoid her and continue doing his job. She still tried to follow him, asking him questions. Diplomat was hoping that he would break and give him a clue to what was going. Then out of the blue, the camera turned to Todd Gross as he walked out of his offices and up to Kelly. He had his hands in his pockets. Kelly turned around, surprised.

"Hello, Kelly. We meet again. Before you start saying anything funny, especially considering the world we live in, just know that it is time for new investments.

Kelly shoved the microphone in Todd's face. He looked down at it, then back up at Kelly. He smiled at the camera. He continued,

"Gross Enterprises is moving up in the world, I suggest you follow. You have nothing to worry about. That is all. Thank you."

"But Mr. Gross," Kelly started, "What do you plan to…"

Todd waved Kelly away as his limousine drove up and parked in front of him. His driver got out of the car, walked over and opened the door for him. Todd stepped inside and they drove off. Kelly turned back to the camera.

"Is this a good deal or raw deal? Only time will tell. I'm Kelly Yamamoto signing off for channel 7 news.

The Diplomat raised one eyebrow and turned off the TV.

"So, what do you think?" Maverick said on the other line.

Diplomat answered, "Why would he do something like that? Hmmm, I'm going to check for Secret Scroll activity on the computer."

"Okay." Maverick said, "Call me if you need me."

"Ten four." Diplomat replied and hung up the phone. That short interview gave him a little more information to work with. Now it was time to put a plan in action.

10

It took a special kind of person to volunteer at Children's Hospital. It could sometimes take a toll on a person to see children suffer from so many different illnesses. Malik, also known as Modern Day, was just that type of person. He was a barber by trade, being part owner in a barbershop called Nice Nelson's but in his spare time, he volunteered at Children's Hospital near downtown Los Angeles. He often provided the kids with much needed haircuts. He felt it was the least he could do.

Today, he was with one of his favorite kids, Mikey, a leukemia patient. Mikey was one of the rare kids who still had some hair growth despite going through chemo and radiation treatments. Malik had just finished shaving some stars into the side of his head and was walking with him as he rolled to his room. Mikey turned around in his chair and faced Malik.

"Race ya?"

"Got it." Malik replied as he grabbed the handles of Mikey's wheelchair. They started zooming through the hallways. As Malik picked up speed, Mikey began to laugh and threw up his hands.

"WEEEEEEEEEEEEEE!!!!!" Mikey screamed as Malik made a sharp turn. Mikey grew silent as his wheelchair almost collided with Mikey's main nurse, Ms. McKey. Ms. McKey stared at Mikey and then at Malik. She narrowed her eyes and shook her head.

"What am I going to do with you two? Malik, how many times have I told you not to push these children around in the hospital like that? This isn't NASCAR. Mikey needs his rest. Now, could you please roll him back to his room safely?"

Malik nodded and reached behind him. Unzipping the top part off his backpack, he reached inside and pulled out a pack of donuts. He pulled one out and handed it to Ms. McKey.

"Yes Nurse McKey, here is a doughnut for you."

Nurse McKey shook her head again and walked off.

"You can't butter me up that way. Just be careful next time." She said as she rounded the corner.

"We will." Malik yelled after her. The two waited a moment.

"Is the coast clear?" Mikey asked.

Malik looked around the corner. "Yes."

Mikey winked at him and the two dashed through the halls once again.

"Vroom, vroom!" Malik yelled as they raced around one more corner and approached the playroom. Just as they were about to enter in, Malik tripped over some scrubs that were hanging on the door and he crashed to the floor, taking Mikey with him. Malik leaned over and looked at Mikey who was sitting on the floor, near his wheelchair.

"Mikey, Mikey are you okay?"

Mikey looked over at Malik and nodded his head. They both started to laugh.

"I guess the nurse does know best. I just learned a valuable lesson."

Mikey nodded his head again, "Are you okay, Mr. Conway? What type of lesson did you learn?"

Malik stood up and helped Mikey into his chair. He pointed to the rules on the wall. "Follow the rules of the area you're in."

Mikey looked up at him and smiled. "I can't believe you still learn lessons Mr. Conway. You're an adult."

"Are you kidding, my little friend? Malik said, "Adults learn every day, just like children."

Malik rolled Mikey into the playroom. It was tough to see so many children suffering from terminal illnesses. He knew that by the end of the year, at least two of the ten children in the room wouldn't be around this time in the next year. He wanted to make sure that they had some magic and fun in their lives.

As they walked in, five other little kids ran up to them. Their voices sounded like music as they asked Malik to tell them one of his famous "K.A.T.H.I.N.S. true stories. A lot of these children grew up watching the Marvel hero movies. He wanted to let them know that real heroes existed and they were human. He also wanted them to believe that they were superheroes to their families also.

Malik rolled Mikey to the middle of the room as the other children gathered around him. Malik sat in front of the captive audience.

"Children, children, calm down. If you all want the truth, I will always give you the truth."

Diana, another little one suffering from Leukemia, sat in front of Malik,

"And Mr. Conway, don't leave out any important stuff." She said.

"Yeah Mr. Conway, tell us about Amdogata." Stevie demanded.

At the sound of Amdogata's name, all of the kids in the room started to boo. Malik laughed.

"Yes, everyone gather closer. I'll get straight to the point, kids. There are evil forces in society, my friends and they must be stopped. That's where the K.A.T.H.I.N.S. come in. They do their best to stop the evil, mean Amdogata."

The kids cheered, Malik continued,

"I want you to picture a man that has access to high tech equipment and the power to manipulate people in high places as well as low."

One of the older boys, Bobby said,

"Wow, Mr. Conway that's deep."

Malik nodded his head. He turned to the other kids. "Before we continue, I wanted to make sure you understood what Bobby meant when he said the word, deep. What he meant was that it has a lot of meaning. Do you understand what I mean by that?"

All the kids nodded their heads. Malik smiled,

"Good."

"As you were saying about the K.A.T.H.I.N.S. stopping evil..." Bobby said, eagerly.

Jessie raised his hand.

"What is evil?"

Malik turned to Jessie, "Good question, Jessie. Evil is when a person does bad things even when they know better. We all live in a beautiful world but sometimes things can make it hard. Amdogata will try to destroy this world because he is not from our planet. He is from Planet Limbo. He hates children like you and will stop at nothing to harm you."

Mikey looked frightened and put his hand to his mouth. "Oh my goodness, Mr. Conway. No!"

Malik gets up and walks over to the window. "Yes, yes, unfortunately this is true. But there is one problem for him, that is a good thing for us. This evil being cannot reach his full power here on earth. You will never see Amdogata in his purest form."

"Why not, Mr. Conway?" Cindy asked.

Malik walked over to Cindy and kneeled down. "In a nutshell, Cindy; The Powers That Be. They give the K.A.T.H.I.N.S. wisdom in their time of need. They also give the K.A.T.H.I.N.S. insight. Let me tell you a story"

Malik walked back to his chair. The children are captivated, eager to hear what was next. Malik continued,

"The leader of the K.A.T.H.I.N.S., Young Octane, guides five other soldiers that were specially trained to stop Amdogata."

What type of training is this, Mr. Conway?" Mikey asked.

"You ask a lot of good questions Mikey." Malik said, "I like that. What Mikey is doing kids, is asking for more knowledge. If you don't understand something, don't be afraid to ask someone."

Mikey smiled. Malik winced slightly as the K.A.T.H.I.N.S. Communicator began to vibrate silently. Malik turned back to the kids and smiled.

"I'm sorry my friends but I have to go. I have business elsewhere. I'll see you all again."

The kids waved and said goodbye as Malik stood up and began to walk to the door. Dianna stood up and walked over to him.

"You do your part, don't you Mr. Conway?"

Malik turned around and smiled. "You can believe that, princess. Please believe it."

Dianna smiled and hugged Malik. He turned around and waved to the other kids before entering into the hallway. He walked past Nurse McKey while she is eating her doughnut.

"Bye Nurse McKey. I hope you are enjoying that doughnut. You know Ms. McKey, I bought it from the best spot in town."

Nurse McKey wiped her mouth off with a napkin and laughed.

"Malik, you are a decent person. Playful, but a good man."

Malik smiled as he walked down the hallway and exited the hospital. Once he was safely in his car, he was in Modern Day mode. He opened his K.A.T.H.I.N.S. Communicator. Alkaline's face appeared on the screen.

"Hello, Modern Day."

"Good afternoon, Alkaline. What's going on?" Modern Day responded

"I've been having weird dreams all day today. I sense the presence of Amdogata."

Modern Day was startled, "Really? How?"

"Well, Diplomat just told us that the billionaire Todd Gross has just purchased over thirty percent of San Fernando Valley today as well as a lot of land in the Santa Monica Mountains. With the dreams that I've been having, Malik, this doesn't look good, he, he..."

"What is it you're trying to tell me?" Modern Day asked.

"Diplomat has been telling me that Todd has been moving all types of machinery into that mountain. I know what this means Malik and you should too."

Modern Day snapped his fingers. "Scrolls! He has located the Secret Scrolls."

Modern Day put the K.A.T.H.I.N.S. earpiece in his ear before starting his car.

"Possibly. I'm taking Space Hawk to the K.A.T.H.I.N.S. Headquarters right after I finish this press release. The Diplomat is gathering as much information as he can." Alkaline replied.

Modern Day nodded his head. "K.A.T.H.I.N.S. over and out."

Modern Day took off his earpiece and threw into his glove compartment. He took off in his car and drove towards the San Fernando Valley.

"Well it looks like it might be time for another adventure."

After about 20 minutes, Modern Day was on PCH, with the Pacific Ocean to his left. The sun was shining brightly. He felt its warmth on his face. He glanced out of the window with confidence.

"We did it before; we'll do it again. Goodwill never loses as long as the K.A.T.H.I.N.S. have something to do with it. I have to get to Octane's job pronto. Amdogata must be stopped."

11

Palos Verdes was one of those quiet
hillside communities that overlooked the Pacific
Ocean. It was a good place to grow up; safe and
secluded from the rest of the world. The sunsets
were breathtaking and it was a stone's throw
away from Hermosa and Redondo Beach,
where April and her friends would spend hours
on the water, surfing and paddle boarding.
Today, however, April was finishing the press
release for the K.A.T.H.I.N.S. Campaign.

She finally pulled herself out of bed and
away from her dreams. She had been in front of
her computer for hours prior to talking on the
phone with Diplomat and Modern Day. She
needed to take a break. She looked at her clock.
It was one in the afternoon. It was definitely
time to grab something to eat.

She stood up and walked out of her home
office. She proceeded downstairs to the kitchen
to grab herself a snack. She had to remember to
eat sometimes. She wouldn't be at her best, if
she didn't. Just as she was fixing herself a snack
of blue corn tortilla chips and mango papaya
salsa, she heard her K.A.T.H.I.N.S.
communicator buzz. April ran over to the

counter and looked at the message. It just had two simple words on it.

"It's time."

April nodded her head. She took two more bites of her snack and then ran downstairs to the basement where Space Hawk was located. Her basement was actually about 300 feet into the cliffs. Space Hawk was her baby. It was a multifunctional vehicle that operated on land, air and sea. She liked going underwater the best. Living near the ocean all of her life sparked her interest in marine biology. The ocean was so amazing to her that she double majored in communications and marine biology. Using Space Hawk indulged her inner Jacque Cousteau.

As she was buckling into Space Hawk, she pressed the controls to give her invisibility as she prepared to blast from under the ocean. Before taking off, she looked at the sea life that swam in front of her and smiled. It always calmed her down before any mission.

"Time to rock and roll." April said to herself as she pressed the ignition key and took off. This was the time that she got the chance to embrace her alter ego, Alkaline. Alkaline was strong, she was fierce and brave. She was the complete opposite of April who had grown up with a silver spoon in her mouth and a golden rattle in her hand.

She heard the engines engage and felt the familiar force of being thrown back into her seat as she blasted through the ocean. She was navigating herself to the top of the water, making sure not to emerge near any surfers or boats. Moments later, she was safely in the air.

As she reached 10,000 feet, she turned on her communication screen. She dialed and Diplomat's face appeared shortly after.

"I'm heading towards the K.A.T.H.I.N.S. Headquarters. What do you mean by it's time?" Alkaline asked.

"It's just time, Alkaline. All hands need to be on deck." Diplomat answered.

"I've been having crazy dreams lately and coupling that with the strange orbs that flew into the Santa Monica Mountains, I'm thinking that Amdogata might've finally reached earth's realm. Or at least, something connected to him." Alkaline said.

"That could be true. Once you get here, we will have time to figure something out and

come up with a game plan What is your ETA?"
Diplomat replied.

"I'm travelling at almost Mach 1, so I
should be there within the next ten minutes or
so. I have the invincibility shields up and…"
Her voice trailed off.

Something caught Alkaline's attention
out of the corner of her eye. It looked like a
stealth fighter and it was flying aggressively
close to her. She knew she had her shields up
but still… It looked as if it was about to attack
her.

"What, in the … "

Alkaline and Diplomat then heard a
voice. It permeated the walls of Space Hawk.
The voice sounded familiar.

"What a simpleton. Where did you get
your pilot's license? Pluto?"

"Oh my God. Who is that?" Alkaline
asked.

"I don't know." Diplomat said. "Let me
try to help you." He then leaned over and began
to radio the other K.A.T.H.I.N.S.
communicators.

"Let me zero in on you." Diplomat continued.

"What? Diplomat, I can't hear you." Alkaline yelled at the screen.

"I can't find you. Your signal is being scrambled. I'm trying to get a lock on the UFO."

"I can do it." Alkaline said. Trying to stay calm, she pushed a few buttons on the screen and a picture of the aircraft appeared. All of the information came up shortly after. It was called the Grim Machine II. It was owned by Gross Industries and its coordinates were 34°17'14"N 118°26'20"W. She repeated the numbers to Diplomat. The plane zoomed past her.

"I knew it!" Alkaline exclaimed. "That thing is headed for San Fernando Valley. I've got to investigate this situation." She maneuvered the plane to follow the Grim Machine. Her heart was sinking and her stomach was in knots. She had mixed feelings about what she was doing. She didn't want to be lured into something without back up.

Diplomat tried to stop her. "No, Alkaline! We don't know what you're up against. Octane wouldn't approve of this at all."

"I know but still... I..." Alkaline stopped in mid-sentenced. Her eyes widened as she saw the Grim Machine II turn around and start coming directly towards her. She tried to move out the way when the aircraft started shooting at her.

"He saw I was following him. How can he see me?" Alkaline said.

"Get out of there!" Diplomat yelled.

Alkaline smiled to herself. This is one of the moments she had been waiting for. It was time to get it done. "Well, I guess it's time for him to feel the power of Space Hawk.

Alkaline shifted gears causing Space Hawk to zoom high into the clouds, past the planes and the jets. Where it was almost always perpetual night. Grim Machine II was following close behind. Where did he get this technology from?
"I've got to get this thing away from the city." Alkaline said to Diplomat.

"Do that. We will lock you in and send reinforcements." Diplomat replied.

She felt the engines hit full throttle as she fired shots out the back of Space Hawk. She had already passed Mach 1, now she was hitting Mach 3. Grim Machine stayed hot on her tail.

"Holy moly, that thing is still on my tail." Alkaline said as she turned on her K.A.T.H.I.N.S. C.B. She spoke into the microphone.

"What do you want from me? I mean you no harm."

Todd Gross's voice came over the speakers. "Your soul, my child. All of your hopes and dreams."

She heard a couple beeps. Alkaline instinctively looked into her rear-view camera. She saw a blast of light and fire as Todd shot a missile towards Space Hawk. Alkaline had only seconds to move out of the way of the missile. She still didn't understand how he could see her. She took a few seconds to compose herself before responding back.

"Well it's not for sale, I'm part of The K.A.T.H.I.N.S."

Alkaline leaned over and pressed a
couple more buttons on the console. The screen
in front of her said "The K.A.T.H.I.N.S. Mode"
She pushed another button and grabbed the
wheel. She immediately started to fly backward.
Space Hawk morphed and shifted with Alkaline
facing the back of the ship. She was heading
towards Todd. She pressed a few more buttons
and returned fire. Grim Machine II moved out
of the way but not before the aircraft was hit on
the right wing.

She could hear Todd over the speakers.
He was panicking. "Ahh! Mayday, Mayday.
I'm going down." He screamed.

Alkaline watched as the Grim Machine II
spiraled towards earth. She didn't panic. They
weren't out of Earth's atmosphere so it
wouldn't cause a catastrophe if it crashed into
Earth. However, she wanted to make sure, so
she decided to follow. The Grim Machine II
was spinning as it came headed towards the
Santa Monica Mountains, ultimately crashing
into them. Before impact, Alkaline saw a tiny
figure eject itself out of the aircraft. It landed
safely into some bushes about one hundred
yards away. It was Todd, waving his fist in the
air.

"He won't be doing anything for a while." Alkaline said to herself. She turned the vehicle around and proceeded to head back to the K.A.T.H.I.N.S. headquarters. She had to have Maverick access the damage that was done to Space Hawk. Just before she was able to fully complete her turn, she saw Todd reach into his pocket and pull out a phone. He put it to his ear and pointed to Space Hawk. She heard him over her speakers.

"Get her. I want her now!" He screamed.

"What?" She said to herself. Then her heart dropped as she heard the sound of jet engines. She looked in her rearview camera and watched in horror as six drones flew out of the mountain and headed towards her ship. They assembled into a hexagon formation and began to fire at her. She turned around and tried not to panic.

"Well, I guess it's time to go." She said as she pushed Space Hawk to full throttle.

She frantically tried to dial one of her K.A.T.H.I.N.S. comrades to help her out of this jam but she was just too clumsy. She had to calm down and focus. She knew she had to get away. Space Hawk was capable of going Mach 5, which would cause multiple loud booms to

be heard across California. With the world
being the way it was at the moment; she didn't
want to cause people to be alarmed or scared.
To bring peace was part of her job and she took
it seriously.

"I don't know how Diplomat and I are
going to explain this one. Alkaline watched the
red lasers fly through the sky and disappeared
into the clouds. And it frightened her. She had
to make sure that the drones only fired at her.
She didn't want to risk them shooting at any
passenger planes. She was wondering when the
Air force would come and manage the
unauthorized aircrafts but then she remembered
that Gross Industries provided the military with
most of their weaponry.

"Shoot." She said as she continued to
maneuver away from the laser blasts. "I have to
lead them to a higher altitude."

With the push of a couple buttons,
Alkaline turned Space Hawk towards the sky
and switched to K.A.T.H.I.N.S. speed.

"Buzzfeed will figure out how to explain
this. We will clean it up later." She said to
herself as she was thrown back in her seat.
Space Hawk sped through the sky and she heard
the sonic boom as she left the android troops

behind. Once she was in the higher elevations, she righted her position and headed towards the K.A.T.H.I.N.S. Headquarters.

12

Maria just stared at the live feed on Channel Five. Six drones were in the sky, shooting lasers into the air. To the viewer, it looked like they were shooting into a void, nothingness, however Maria knew, and she was alarmed. Willie, Maria and the rest of the dining area watched the scene unfold in silence. She knew that once her shift was over, she would have to make her way to the K.A.T.H.I.N.S. headquarters as soon as possible. She glanced down at her watch. Thirty minutes to go. Then it was show time.

Breakfast was over and Maria ran to the parking lot. She was in Merciful mode as she jumped onto her motorcycle and headed out to the San Fernando. She always took her motorcycle because it allowed her to maneuver through the bumper-to-bumper L.A. traffic. From the 110, down Arroyo Parkway, she found herself on the 210 Freeway. She tried to reason out what happened. She didn't have time to check the blogs or the news outlets. She just had to get around the other K.A.T.H.I.N.S. so they could devise a game plan. Time was of the essence.

Her head was filled with crazy thoughts. "I know Amdogata is behind this, I can feel his presence."

She was almost there.

****

Todd was pissed and the world always felt his wrath when he was angry. Although, he considered himself a philanthropist and altruistic, he also came up with some of his greatest inventions when he was mad. They caused destruction. They caused pain to others, but he reasoned that as long as they kept him and his shareholders wealthy and on the top of the food chain, that was all that mattered to him. He would be able to clean up the carnage later.

His newest stealth aircraft was amazing, but it was still nothing compared to the Space Hawk. He wondered who created this technology. It had to be from another world. He had to get his hands on it. He knew he would. It was just a matter of time.

Todd sat at a round table looking at the mountainside property he had just purchased. He was still sore from the crash from a few hours ago. He landed safely with no problems. He wondered if it was his ego that was bruised or if it really was his body. He tapped his fingers on the table and then heard ringing over the speakers. He pressed a few buttons and a video screen descended from the ceiling. A few moments later, Amdogata appeared on the monitor. He wondered how he was able to transmit over Earth's technology.

"Is everything going to plan, Todd?" Amdogata asked.

"Yes Amdogata. Everything is perfect. They are digging under the mountain now. But tell me what are you looking for, what is going ...?"

Amdogata slammed his hand down. A loud clap echoed through the air and red lightning flashed behind him. Todd was scared, but he was taught to never show fear. Must. Not. Show. Fear. Todd kept his face composed. Amdogata continued,

"Silence, you mortal! You are nothing. Just do what I've requested and you will be rewarded with what you want."

"Okay, if you say ..." Todd tried to interject,

"Silence!"

Todd quieted down. He had nothing else
to say. It was going to be a long day.

****

Maria decided to take a quick detour.
She just had to investigate this herself. So,
through the mountains she went until she found
her destination. It was time to watch. She used
to hike through these mountains so she knew all
the little backways and places to hide. She
stationed herself in a hidden area and pulled out
her binoculars. She saw digging and movement.
Mr. Gross was making quite the commotion.

"Wow. Mr. Gross's equipment trucks
have weapons and sensors. I'm picking up
heavy frequencies from that area." She said to
herself. Maria heard her K.A.T.H.I.N.S.
Communicator ring. She immediately silenced
it. She didn't want to bring attention to herself.
She took it out of her pocket and opened it.
Modern Day was paging her.

"Hello, Merciful. What are you doing?
Where are you?" Modern Day asked. "Have
you been watching the news?"

"I'm in the valley right now.

"What? Have you talked to Octane?" He asked.

"I don't like to bother him at work. Now, look I'm going to take a closer look. I'll call you when I'm inside.

Modern Day's eyes widened in shock. "Merciful... Please..."

Merciful closed the communicator and placed it back in her pocket. She picked up the binoculars and continued to watch. "

"She could handle this." She thought to herself. She heard the sound of branches being moved behind her. She didn't really pay it any mind. It may have been a bird or some other little animal. But it wasn't. It had a chance to sneak up on her. She didn't react in time.

It was too late.

13

The beautiful location of the K.A.T.H.I.N.S. Headquarters helped to keep the Diplomat sane. It was hidden in plain sight. A little gem of a place that their fathers had bought for them, a long time ago. Well, the word "little" was not the proper description for the building. It was large, constructed of marble walls and windows. It soaked up sunshine and glowed with the moonlight. It had secret entrances and exits. It was historical. It was... perfect.

The Diplomat hadn't left his office since eight in the morning. He was still trying to find answers to the questions that have been plaguing him. As the day developed, he began to question more as he heard about the attack on Alkaline as well as the news coverage of unidentified aircrafts shooting lasers into the sky. The story has since been spun with reporters saying that the event was a part of a movie that was being shot in the area. Since then, the hubbub about it has calmed down.

Maverick was on the side monitor as Diplomat typed on the computer. He slammed his hands on the keyboard and pushed himself away from the desk.

"I knew it!" He shouted.

"Another Secret Scroll, huh?"

"Yep, I'm calling Octane. You call the others. Earth is depending on us."

Maverick nodded his head, "I'm on it, K.A.T.H.I.N.S. out."

****

The ride to the K.A.T.H.I.N.S. headquarters was a relatively smooth one, compared to what happened moments earlier. She slowed down to cruise once she approached the fortress that was nestled in the La Vina Mountains. She pressed a few buttons and the mountains opened up, allowing her to fly inside of the garage that was located underneath the compound. She sat inside Space Hawk for a few moments to compose herself before jumping out.

Alkaline pressed a few buttons on her console. The combination of commands would allow the ship to self-diagnose itself to find out what areas needed repair. If anything was damaged, Maverick would be able to fix it. As the vehicle was inspecting itself, she unbuckled her seat belt and discharged from the vehicle.

She did a quick glance around the ship before walking over to the elevator.

When Alkaline finally reached the mezzanine area of the headquarters, she ran into the office where Diplomat was sitting and conversing with Maverick on the monitor. She sat next to Diplomat who turned to her.

"Todd Gross attacked me."

Diplomat just stared at her and nodded his head. "It's all starting to make sense.

14

It was lunchtime and the kids were eating. Patrick watched them with a smile on his face. He glanced down at his watch, then back at his colleagues.

"Will you look at the time? It's time for my break. I'll see you all in an hour." Patrick said as he stood up. His colleagues waved good bye to him as he made his way through the playground towards the staff parking lot. Patrick got inside and drove out, heading over to go see his usual lunch date at UCLA Medical Center. His grandmother.

As Patrick drove through the streets of west Los Angeles, he began to reminisce about a memory of his grandmother chasing him through a parking lot. He was six years old and they just finished grocery shopping. As his grandma was pushing the basket, Patrick got away and began to run through the parking lot. His grandmother let go of the cart and ran as fast as she could after him. When she finally caught up to him, she grabbed his little hand and pulled him towards her. He looked up at her, laughing. Patrick snapped out of his daze, just as he was approaching the entrance to the hospital.

He parked and got out of the car, but just before leaving the car, he reached into the backseat to grab a dozen roses. Patrick shut the door behind him and walked to the front of the hospital. Patrick walked past the front desk with a face like stone. He made his way to the elevator and once inside, pressed the button for the fifth floor. It was always hard to see her this way. His strong, amazing grandmother. The backbone of his family.

The elevator stopped and chimed. The doors opened to the fifth-floor lobby. He smiled at the nurses as he walked to room 503. Patrick took a deep breath. He stood there for a moment before finally opening the door. The place was full of sunlight just like his grandma. Her room always smelled of lilies, her favorite scent. Patrick's face lit up as he walked toward the bed of one of his greatest mentors. He moved his arm to reveal the bouquet of fresh roses as he sat the vase on the table next to her bed. She was resting, her chest slowly moving up and down. Patrick took a seat next to his sickly grandmother. He kissed her gently on the forehead. She opened up her eyes and smiled.

"Hello, gramma. How have you been doing?"

"Fine, baby. How have you been doing with those kids?" She said. Her voice was gaining more strength as she sat up in the hospital bed. Patrick reached over and propped up her pillows behind her back.

"Is that better?" Patrick asked.

"Much better, baby." His grandma responded.

Patrick sighed deeply, "I've been taking good care of my students. It's crazy, grandma. I love the children so much. I don't want anything to happen to them. They're so tiny, you know?"

"That's what I like to hear, honey. Those kids are the future and you play an important role in their lives. Sweetheart, we all must do our part in this normal society. Not just for those children in your program, but also for the children throughout the nation. The kids need you and believe it or not you need them too."

"Well I'm there for them, gramma."

"I know you are, honey." She said

"So what are we having for lunch today?" Patrick asked.

Grandma leaned over and checked the tray that was on her bedside table. There were some peas and carrots, turkey slices and some applesauce.

"The usual. Filet mignon, garlic mashed potatoes with sautéed asparagus."

"Must be nice." Patrick responded, smiling.

"I know it's time for you to get back to work soon. I know how that L.A. traffic heading east can be."

"Yea. It's true. I'll see you tomorrow at the same time, champ." Patrick said and stood up.

"Put the roses with all of the rest of the ones you've given me." She said. Patrick leaned over and kissed his grandmother on the cheek. He then picked up the vase and placed it near the window. He then walked over to the door. He waved good bye to her one more time as she turned on the TV and leaned back into her bed. He felt relieved as he closed the door behind him.

The K.A.T.H.I.N.S. Communicator rung as he approached his car. Once, inside and buckled in, he connected the device to his radio and answered it. He pulled out of the parking lot. He was in Octane mode.

"Talk to me?" Octane said.

Diplomat appeared on the screen. "There are Secret Scrolls in the valley."

Octane shook his head. "Any indication of Amdogata?"

"I don't know." Diplomat replied, "But he could have something to do with that billionaire doing all this random stuff story that's been going around."

Octane made a right turn to get on the 405 freeway. "Explain."

"Well, today multi-billionaire, Todd Gross, purchased over thirty percent of the valley where the Scrolls are located. Hold on, I'm getting a call from Modern Day."

The screen went black.

"It is Amdogata, for sure. what does he have up his sleeve? What is he plotting?" Octane said to himself. After a few moments, Diplomat appeared on the screen again. He looked stressed. Looking away, he ran his hand across his face. He then turned back to the screen.

"Octane, Alkaline was attacked by some type of machine that was able to detect Space Hawk while it was in invisible mode."

"What? Is she okay?" Octane asked.

Alkaline's face jumped onto the screen. She waved at Octane.

"I'm fine." She said. "A little shaken, but I'm good."

Diplomat continued, "And get this; it had the same logos that Gross's equipment trucks have. Plus, it gets worse. Maverick told me today that Merciful went snooping around in the mountains and now we can't get a hold of her.

"Is she all right?"

"We don't know." Alkaline said, "I'm worried about her."

Octane shook his head as he got off the ten freeway at Western. "What is a matter with that girl?"

Diplomat shook his head and shrugged. "I don't know."

"Listen, tell the rest of the K.A.T.H.I.N.S. to stand by. I get off work in two hours." Octane replied.

"What about Maria?" Alkaline asked.

"If you get in contact with her, tell her to get out of there as soon as possible. I don't know if Amdogata is behind this. If he is, it might be trouble, not only for her, but the entire K.A.T.H.I.N.S. organization as well. I'm going back to work. K.A.T.H.I.N.S. out!

Octane parked his car in the parking lot. Before he was able to get out of the car, he was suddenly overcome by the voices of The Powers That Be. It caused him to feel dizzy, as if he was being taken over and transported to another place. It was part of his duty as the leader of the K.A.T.H.I.N.S. but he hated it. He was afraid that this would happen while he was driving or around the children and that it would cause harm. It has been happening to him since he was eleven years old but he was always alone. He had been lucky.

"Powers That Be!" Octane said to himself as he closed his eyes and leaned against his car to steady himself. When he opened his eyes, he found himself in the Sanctuary, in the Latter World. In a gold room, with the stories of all the worlds engraved on the walls, only being lit by a single fire that was placed in the corner of the room. Octane stood there and waited to be addressed.

A loud voice bellowed. It echoed through the walls, causing the stones to ripple. "K.A.T.H.I.N.S., it is just the beginning. You will be tested like you have never been tested before. Amdogata must be defeated. Not only for the sake of the momentum, but for the sake of The Latter World as well! Remember, Young Octane, This Is Where the Power Lies!"

Octane raised his fist in a salute. "And that's just that real. Just that pure,".

He felt dizzy again. When he opened his eyes, he was back at Western Boulevard. He looked at his watch. It was 11:30AM. Right on time. He had to finish his day.

15

Just before it was too late, Merciful turned around to see a coyote gingerly walk towards her. She stared at it for a moment before slowly standing up to her full height, trying to scare it away. They stared at each other for a few more minutes before the coyote ran off into the bushes. She breathed a sigh of relief before gathering up her things.

"Close one. I have to be more careful" She said to herself as she got on her bike. She put on her helmet and pressed a couple buttons on her bike. Before her eyes, SD1 transformed into K.A.T.H.I.N.S. mode. She sped down the mountain trail. As she bobbed and weaved through the trees and shrubbery, she thought to herself,

"I have to get to the bottom of this. Something strange is definitely going on."

****

Todd Gross really hated to be around humans sometimes. They were unpredictable, greedy and downright self-centered at times. And it all comes from the same place, insecurity. People do the dumbest things out of insecurity. That's why there were wars, why people lied and why people were just really, really nasty to each other. It disgusted Todd to no end. Although, constructing war machines is what initially provided the Gross family with their immense wealth, Todd felt it was his duty to bring some change, some peace to Earth and he felt that helping Amdogata acquire the Secret Scrolls would do just that.

"There would be no more arguing over the small things, no more wars over ego." Todd thought as he sat at the roundtable in his office. "There would be one ruler, one higher power, and that would be Amdogata."

That is why he felt more at home with the Androids. They had no concept of selfishness or hatred. All they knew was to serve, just like Amdogata's army. He was still aching from the little tumble he sustained while flying earlier that day. He would have to work out the kinks of his pilot suit.

Todd often compared himself to the fictional character, Tony Starks. They both had similar backgrounds, and just like Ironman, he wanted to do good in the world. They just had different ways of going about it. He closed his eyes and leaned back in his chair, stretching out his legs. Moments later, he heard a knock on the door.

Come in." Todd said.

A metallic voice said to him, "Mr. Gross, we have an intruder on the premises."

Todd opened up his eyes and sat up. He turned around and looked at his favorite Android, Milo, a smooth, silvery, seven-foot tall humanoid. The eyes were coal black with a small, gunmetal gray slit for a mouth. He didn't want his creations to look too human. That would creep him out.

"What? Capture whoever it is at once." Todd demanded.

Milo bowed slightly. "Yes, Mr. Gross."

"Oh yes, Milo and one more thing."

"Yes, Mr. Gross."

Todd leaned forward. "No excuses!"

Milo nodded his head. "Yes, Mr. Gross."

Milo left the room. Todd turned around and faced the mountains again. His conference room phone rang. Todd leaned over and pushed the accept button. The monitor came down from the ceiling. Once it was fully turned on, Amdogata appeared. Todd stared at the screen.

"Is there a problem, Todd?" Amdogata asked.

"No, Amdogata. Not at all."

Amdogata shook his head. A thunderclap was heard in the distance. Todd composed himself. "You're lying, Todd. Don't lie to me. I can tell when you're lying."

"Milo, my Android, will take care of the problem, he ..." Todd said.

Amdogata slammed his hand down on the table. Todd plugged his ears. The walls shook as the sound echoed throughout Todd's office. "No! You, Mr. Gross, you will take care of the problem. Get down there, now!"

Todd was now completely frightened. He couldn't hide it anymore. His voice shook as he answered Amdogata,

"Yes, Amdogata. Yes."

16

Merciful felt like she was going nowhere. She didn't find any of the evidence that she needed to tie Todd Gross and his company to the strange happenings that were going on. This was her calling, her duty that she had to fulfill. Her and her friends were chosen to protect the Earth's realm and the Secret Scrolls. Every single one of the K.A.T.H.I.N.S. studied and memorized them. She stopped her bike for a moment. She had to think.

She began to wonder if there was something wrong with her directions, because she saw what looked to be men in metallic suits moving things in and out of the mountainside. She was sure that she was riding in the right direction, however everywhere she turned, she just ran into more trees and bushes. She didn't eat that much today, but that shouldn't affect her to where she was beginning to hallucinate. Those days were over.

"Oh well." She said to herself. "Must keep going. I can't give up." So, she jumped back on her bike and kept going.

As she rounded a corner, something weird and terrifying caught her eye. It was a glint of silver and black. Merciful turned her head around for a quick glance. It was a silver robot. It had a strange but familiar logo on its forehead, and it was holding a weird-shaped gun. It was pointing the weapon straight at her. The Android fired and a thick red beam shot out, narrowly missing her. She ducked just in time.

"Oh My God. Oh My God. Oh My God." Merciful said to herself as she kicked her motorcycle into high gear. "That narrowly missed me. I gotta kick it up to the next level."

She was soon surrounded. Silver robots holding the same weird guns seemed to come out of nowhere. They all took aim at her.

"Maria... MOVE." She screamed to herself as she took off. As she rode through the mountain paths, Merciful pushed the bike to full throttle. Turning right and then left, trying her best to dodge the red lasers that were being shot at her. She contemplated firing back but she knew that it would rob her of some of her power and she needed to make it back to the city. She bobbed and weaved through the paths, as the red lasers knocked bushes and trees into her path. However, because of the design of her vehicle and her speeds of over two hundred miles per hour, she was able to clear them without slowing down.

Merciful came upon a dead end at the bottom of the mountain. She was becoming scared but she had to fight through the fear and press on. As she quickly approached the mountain, she pressed a few buttons on her bike handle and initiated the missile launcher. Using her helmet, she connected with SD1 to identify the best place to shoot the missile that would minimize damage to other life and property. The helmet locked into the base of the mountain three meters east. Merciful tapped the side of her helmet and she felt her bike move forward as the missile was ejected from the front of SD1.

In a matter of seconds, a ten-foot hole formed in the side of the mountain, with fire encompassing the path. It lit the way to other side of the mountain where she could see the 101 freeway. She was home free, just a couple more miles. She pressed a few more buttons on her bike and initiated the force field. She zoomed through the explosion, fully protected. The flames surrounded her but she remained untouched. The heat from the blast created beautiful marble-like sheets within the mountain walls.

"Beautiful." She thought as she rode through. Then a warm feeling overtook her and she felt like she was floating. It was the same feeling she would get whenever she was near the Secret Scrolls.

"Secret Scrolls, oh my! They're here and they are trying to steal them." She said to herself. She looked to the left and lo and behold, she saw more robots, through the flickering flames, digging into the mountain wall. The wall gave off a light blue glow. Merciful pressed the side of her helmet again; activating the voice-activated K.A.T.H.I.N.S. Communicator.

She screamed into the communicator, "Attention all K.A.T.H.I.N.S., I've located the Scrolls and from the way it looks, Amdogata is definitely involved. This has to be the work of Amdo ... uhhh!"

She felt herself get knocked off her bike. "Thank God, I wore my helmet." She thought as she watched SD1 ride to the other side of the mountain. She wouldn't know how to explain that to the team. She heard Diplomat's voice on the communicator.

"Merciful? Where are you?" He asked, frantically.

She was unable to answer. She hit the ground with a thud and the world went all black.

The Grim Machine series was a work of art. There were dozens of machines in the arsenal, ranging from spacecrafts, planes and helicopters, to cars, motorbikes and boats and everything in between. It was something that he developed, that not even the military could get their hands on. When he found the location of the Secret Scrolls, Todd considered this the perfect time to test out the machines. The spacecraft had a few kinks that needed to be worked out but the mini helicopter, a one-man plane equipped with claws and missile launchers proved to work quite efficiently.

Once the Androids locked in on the intruder's whereabouts, Todd used their coordinates to pinpoint the exact place where he would make his move. Flying into the mountainside, he was able to push the trespasser off of their vehicle and throw them to the ground. While the helicopter was in hover mode, Todd jumped out. He ran over to her and kneeled down. He felt around her neck.

"Good." He said to himself, "She still has a pulse. She's just unconscious."

He then leaned down and picked her up off the ground. He placed her in the claws and climbed back into the helicopter. Before he was able to take off, he summoned two of his Androids to come over. They ran over and stood in front of Merciful.

"Dayton, retrieve the motorcycle and destroy it at once, you pathetic piece of machinery."

Dayton nodded his head, "Yes, sir. I'm sorry we have failed you. We shouldn't have let her get this far into the mountain."

"It's okay. Nobody's perfect." Todd said, gently. "After all, I'm the one who created you."

Todd pushed a couple of buttons. The Android army moved out of the way as he maneuvered the Grim Machine out of the mountain. He flew low, undetected as he made his way back to his headquarters.

"This one might be of some use." He thought to himself. "Amdogata will be pleased."

17

"Mariaaaaa!" Maverick screamed,

"Maria, nooooooo!" Diplomat yelled.

Alkaline was at a loss of words. They all saw everything. She had connected to everyone just before she was knocked off of her bike.

Alkaline finally spoke. "Oh Maria!" was all she could eek out. It was only darkness as she was moved out of the mountain. Through the communicator, they saw that she was being flown to an all-white building that looked to be in the middle of nowhere. However, all of them recognized the logo on the front of the building. It made Maverick's heart stop.

"Octane, did you see what just happened?" Diplomat asked.

****

Octane sat in class, trying to maintain his composure. He saw everything. He wanted to scream and run out the classroom, but he knew he couldn't. He didn't want to startle the kids with any sudden outbursts. As they studied,

Octane looked down at his communicator and typed a message to Diplomat.

"Can you find Merciful's coordinates?"

"I recognize the logo. It's Gross Industries." Maverick said, aloud. They all looked at him. Maverick stood up and walked over to the computer.

"I work for a monster." He continued,

"No." Alkaline interrupted, "You work for the good of humanity."

"I am working on getting the coordinates." Diplomat replied.

Diplomat tried desperately to pull up Merciful's coordinates. He tried every combination he could to locate her. Everything showed to be a dead end.

"Dang it!" Diplomat exclaimed, "I think the communicator must have been damaged when she hit the ground."

"What are we going to do?" Alkaline asked, frantically.

"We will figure this out. In the meantime, we need to protect the scrolls. They were in the mountainside. Maybe we can pull up the location of SD1." Maverick said.

"That, I think I can do." Diplomat replied.

"Please do." Octane typed as he closed the communicator. Octane looked up at the clock. It was 2:00 PM and school was almost over. Just twenty more minutes. He hoped Merciful could last that long.

18

Merciful didn't know how long she had been out. In fact, she didn't remember too much after she was knocked off of SD1. So, she tried to contain her panic when she found herself chained from head to toe in the upright position. The room she was in was all white except for a large, black monitor that was affixed to the wall. There were no windows with only one exit to her right. Her helmet was gone, so there was no way for her to communicate with the rest of the team.

Even though, she was empathetic towards others, she was taught to not show emotion when faced with danger. She was born with a warrior spirit. She stayed silent and stone-faced as Todd walked over to her. He leaned towards her and just stared. She looked through him. He smirked.

"One of the infamous K.A.T.H.I.N.S. You don't have to tell me which one. I really don't care. I just expected something a little bit... different. A little more formidable."

He was trying to get a rise out of her. She continued to stare through him, unwilling to even acknowledge him. Todd continued,

"It's okay. You don't have to say anything to me. You will be talking soon enough."

Todd turned around and walked over to the table. He sat down on one of the chairs and leaned over, pressing a button in the center of the table. The monitor turned on. Amdogata appeared on the screen. Merciful's eyes widened. She knew Amdogata was behind this and she couldn't tell anyone anything.

"Hello, young Merciful. We meet again."

It was then she knew to speak. She had to be without fear.

"Amdogata!" She said with a sneer. "I knew it. I knew you were behind all of this. So, tell me Amdogata, what do you plan to do with the Scrolls. What is ...?"

Amdogata slammed his hand against his throne. Todd plugged his ears as the sound echoed through the room. It caused the chains to shake and Merciful' s ears to ring.

"Silence! I don't have to tell you anything, young Merciful. You are not the ruler of the Latter World. Once I gather all the Secret

Scrolls, I will have the keys to defeating The Powers That Be."

When Merciful recovered, she smirked. Laughing, she said, "Tsk, tsk. You'll never defeat The Powers That Be. Good will always triumph over evil. As long as there is good in the world ..."

Amdogata's eyes narrowed in anger. He stood up from his throne. She could see the pain of a thousand souls in his eyes, lightning and darkness. She was literally staring into the eyes of evil. Merciful refused to look away. He took pleasure in this. He couldn't wait until he owned her soul.

"Silence! Who are you to ...?"
Even with a splitting headache, she had to show her strength and the power that she had within her. At the top of her lungs, she shouted, "I'm a part of the K.A.T.H.I.N.S., Amdogata, Kids at The Heart in Normal Society, and you can rest assured I do my part..."

Amdogata paused and stared at her. Deep within her eyes, he was trying to hypnotize her, to pull information out of her. He tried to draw her into his world. To make her feel the pain of the other worlds, other beings he had conquered and destroyed. She refused to be taken in. She held strong to her mind.

"Yeah, Amdogata; that's right." Merciful continued, "I do my part. What do you do, Amdogata? Use people like Gross to help you succeed with your plans for the Scrolls? Well, you're not going to get away with it. Not this time Amdogata, not this time. Your demise will be simply marvelous."

Todd stared at them both, utterly enthralled. He had never seen anyone stand up to Amdogata the way this young K.A.T.H.I.N.S. did. There must be something about the Scrolls that gave people courage. His mind started to wonder. Should he keep the Scrolls for himself? If he ruled the world, the way he ran his company, Earth would definitely be a better place. However, so that Amdogata wouldn't suspect anything, he would continue to act as his loyal guide. Todd walked up to Merciful. She still stared through him.

"That's who I was attacked by today. the bloody K.A.T.H.I.N.S. What in the name of ...?"

"Silence! You might find out soon enough if you're not careful, you weak, pathetic fool. Have the Scrolls delivered to the secret location in the Amazon. That's when you'll be rewarded, Todd; just like we spoke about. The Scrolls are all that matter to me now, to us now."

The monitor went black and Todd turned to stare at her. Merciful's heart was racing. She knew where they were taking the Scrolls and she couldn't tell anyone about it. She couldn't stop them. Todd turned to her and smiled.

"So now you know the plan, but fortunately for me, you're the only one who knows and you won't be released anytime soon."

Todd walked away, satisfied. The tides were changing and they were in Todd's favor.

19

It slipped Octane's mind that he agreed to volunteer at the youth center after work. Although it was an emergency, he hated breaking promises. As he drove to his next destination, he dialed Diplomat's number on the K.A.T.H.I.N.S. communicator.

"Diplomat, have you been able to find Merciful's coordinates?"

"No, we haven't" Diplomat answered. "We are trying to lock in on SD1 right now, but even that is proving to be difficult. It's like that they have some sort of jammer on or something that is crossing the signals."

"Ask Maverick about the other locators he may have added to the vehicle. SD1 should be near Merciful or at least within a few miles of her."

"Copy that." Diplomat said as the screen went black. Octane was finally at the youth center. He parked and sat in the car for a few moments. He had to get out of K.A.T.H.I.N.S. mode and return to being Mr. Shackelford. A couple deep breaths and he was out of the car, walking up the steps to the youth center. He checked in with the receptionist and walked over to the main room where tutoring was held every Wednesday from four to six pm.

Patrick saw one of his favorite students, Leroy, was waiting for him in the corner of the study room. Leroy was a good kid, brilliant, but he had some problems with reading. When Patrick first met Leroy over four months ago, the child could barely spell his name, but he has watched him blossom since he has been tutoring him. Patrick walked up and sat next to him.

"So what book are you reading today, Leroy?"

Leroy looked up at him with defeat and anger in his eyes. "It's too hard, Mr. Shackelford. I can't do it."

"Can't do what?"

"I can't read it." He wailed.

"Leroy, what did I say about the word, can't?"

Leroy hung his head in shame. He then took a deep breath and looked back up at Patrick. "You said that "can't" should not be in my vocabulary. That I can do anything I set my mind to."

"Exactly." Patrick said and pointed to a word in the book. Leroy's eyes followed.

"It's easy, little one." Patrick continued, "What sound do the letters c and h make when combined?"

"Ch Ch Ch Ch" Leroy said, stuttering.

"You can do it. You have what it takes. I believe in you. Now try again."

"Ch, ch, chain!" Leroy exclaimed.

"You got it, buddy. That's correct."

"I did it, Mr. Shackelford! I did it!" Patrick and Leroy slapped five.

"I knew you could do it! This is what the Youth Service Care Program is here for! Leroy, This Is Where the Power Lies. So, are you ready to read some more words?"

"Yes, I am." Leroy said, beaming.

They studied for another hour.

One of the things Patrick loved about the center was that they balanced work with play. "Children needed a break to just be children." Patrick often thought to himself. "They would be adults soon enough."

Patrick was standing in the playground, watching seven little kids including Leroy, chase each other around. They all sat down and Rosia walked around in a circle, tapping each one of them on the top of their head.

"Eenie, meenie, mynee, moe. Catch a tiger by the toe. If he hollers, let him go. Eenie, meenie, mynee, moe. You are out, Elma."

Elma stood up and pointed at Rosia with a confused look on her face. "Nooooo, that's not how you play this game. You cheated, Rosia.

"Mentirosa! You are a liar, Elma!" Rosia replied back with her hands on her hips.

Elma screamed, "You are a liar. Liar, liar, pants on fire, Rosia." Elma took a step towards Rosia. Rosia put her hands out, ready to push Elma away. The other kids stood up.

"Fight! Fight! Fight!" They chanted as they surrounded the girls.

"Dang." Patrick said as he ran over and stood between the girls.

"Girls, girls what's going on? What is this all about?

Elma pointed at Rosia. "Mr. Shackifo, she's cheating." She screamed.

Rosia responded, "No, she's cheating. Don't look at me. Why are you looking at me?"

Patrick sighed. He could already feel Amdogata's presence on Earth. These girls were usually the best of friends and now they were attacking each other. He had to do something about this. "Hey, hey, hey, my goodness. Rosia. Don't talk to your friend like that. Just calm down."

The girls refused to look at each other. Rosia crossed her arms as Elma stuck her tongue out at her. Patrick scratched his head. Patrick continued,

"I'll settle this fair and square. Everyone sit down and let's try this again."

All the kids sat down and Patrick walked around in a circle, tapping each child on the top of the head. "Eenie, meenie, mynee, moe. Catch a tiger by the toe. If he hollers, let him go. Eenie, meenie, mynee, moe. My mother told me to tell you that you are not it for the rest of your entire life." Patrick's hand rested on Elma's head.

Elma stood up and chased Patrick around. He ran around the circle a few times before sitting in Elma's place.

"Well, Elma you're out fair and square."

Elma nodded her head and stood up. She ran over to the other side of the yard to play on the swings.

"Thank you, Mr. Shackifo."

"Enough of this game." Patrick said to the children as he stood up and walked in front of them. "Let me tell you about the aspects of life. You are the future and the decisions you make will affect all of us. Not just me, not just Elma, but everyone on earth, my little friends."

The kids nodded their heads as they listened to him. They always enjoyed his stories. They made them feel like they could accomplish anything they wanted. The kids sometimes needed to hear that in their lives.

Patrick knew this and made a point to share how they can be heroes in this world. Many of the kids came from poor neighborhoods and broken homes. They weren't exposed to a lot of positivity outside of the center. He always mentioned the K.A.T.H.I.N.S. to them. He wanted to show them that everyday people made a difference. This was the lasting impression that Patrick wanted to leave them. He continued with the story,

"I have Kids at The Heart in Normal Society and because of that, they always do right. Just like you must do right. You shouldn't argue. You shouldn't be mean. You have to be the good in this world. If you are good and you treat people right, cool things will follow you wherever you go. Now go, run and play. Do well for society. I believe you can do it."

Leroy smiled, 'Even me, Mr. Shackifo."

Patrick turned to Leroy and smiled, "Especially you, Leroy."

The whistle blew, which meant it was time to go inside for evening snacks. Patrick waved goodbye as the kids got up and ran towards the small cafeteria on the other side of the yard. Patrick watched them go. "It breaks my heart that this might be the only meal these children eat tonight." Patrick thought to himself, "Why can't the world be different?"

Ms. Agwamagwa, the director of the center, walked over to Patrick and the children. "You really love those kids, don't you, Shackelford?"

Patrick turned to Ms. Agwamagwa and smiled. "Yes I do, Rose. We must do all we can for the kids in normal society."

"It's quitting time, sir. We'll see you next week."

"I'll be here." Patrick said as he went into the back room and picked up his things. As he walked to the reception area of the youth center, Elma waved goodbye to him. He smiled,

"Bye, Elma."

He waved goodbye to the office staff as he made his way to the door. Mr. Johnson, one of the security guards, opened the door for him.

"Bye, Shackelford. See you, Wednesday."

"Bye, Mr. Johnson." Patrick said as he walked through the door. As he walked outside, he was mentally preparing himself for Octane mode. He would need to be on his A-game tonight.

20

Once SD1 drove out of the other side of the mountain, Diplomat was able to lock in on the coordinates.

"Yes!" Diplomat screamed, enthusiastically. "We have locked down Merciful's general location. Now if I type this into our satellite, we will be able to pinpoint the exact area of where she is located so we can rescue her."

"What are the coordinates?" Alkaline asked.

"They are 34°07′13″N 118°55′54″W."

"I'm on it!" Alkaline exclaimed as she typed in the coordinates on her laptop. "Let me know when you get a satellite view of the area."

"Will do." Diplomat responded.

"Are you going to let SD1 be destroyed?" Alkaline asked.

"Yes, I would rather the vehicle be destroyed than to fall in the wrong hands. Gross has her and I don't want to give him any more prototypes that can be used to wage war with other countries. Besides, Maverick can always build us another one." Diplomat said, laughing.

"Good luck with that one." Maverick replied. "I'm ready to rock and rolla when we find Merciful's location."

"We all are." Diplomat said. "But I will initiate detonation if I need to."

Diplomat pressed a couple buttons on his screen. "Detonation initiated."

****

The Androids caught SD1 before it fell over the cliff. Forming into a car, the machines brought the vehicle back to Gross's secret headquarters and placed it on a large table. Milo stood at the front of the table.

"Well you heard the boss, get over there and destroy the motorcycle."

Dayton stood next to Milo. "Let's take it to the Room of Doom; I'm going to have a little fun with this."

He reached over to pick up SD1 when an electrical charge ran through him. Dayton was barely able to pull away. Smoke started to come out of the slits on the side of his head. Milo ran over and checked his temperature gauge.

"You're running at 500 Celsius." Milo said.

"This bike must have some type of alarm." Dayton replied.

Milo walked around the bike, taking extra care in not touching it. "That's one powerful alarm."

"It seems we have a bit of a problem now, don't we? What do we tell the boss?" Dayton asked.

Milo just shrugged.

21

Modern Day was waiting in the parking lot, standing next to High Octane in its full glory. Patrick walked up to Modern Day and slapped him five.

"So we have the big guns?" Patrick asked.

"We're gonna need them. So, are you ready?" Modern Day asked.

"Yup." Octane responded and they drove off.

Octane was silent for a moment as they drove to the K.A.T.H.I.N.S. headquarters.

"What's wrong, my dude?" Modern Day asked.

Octane turned to him. "I got a million thoughts running through my head. Stuff like, man, I wish that life was more simple. What has Maria gotten herself into? Ah, I can't think that way. Amdogata has captured Maria and as the leader of the K.A.T.H.I.N.S., I will come through, not only with her rescue but for the Secret Scrolls as well."

"Yea. We wondered why she went alone too, but at least we know she's dedicated and brave. She was on the front line of trying to stop Amdogata."

"I know, but I just don't want anyone to get really hurt. First Alkaline and now Merciful. This isn't turning out too well."

The dashboard monitor turned on and Diplomat appeared on the screen.

"Maria is in quite a bind. Due to the micro K.A.T.H.I.N.S. cameras that shot out when the SD1 was in trouble, we have surveillance of the area. It's associated with Todd Gross and of course, our nemesis, Amdogata. They have Merciful in a non-descript building that is approximately one mile away from SD1's location.

The screen split and Maverick appeared to the left of Diplomat.

Octane replied, "Maverick, that's where you come in. I want you to take Sky Guardian and retrieve SD1."

"We've already initiated detonation sequence. Well, only if SD1 is tampered with." Diplomat replied.

"Has it been tampered with?" Modern Day asked.

Maverick reached over and typed into a computer that was located to the right of his monitor. Maverick shook his head and then turned back to the screen.

"No, it hasn't. I will deactivate detonation."

"Thank you." Octane said. "So here is the game plan. I will rescue Merciful. Maverick, you and Alkaline will have to get the Scrolls. When Modern Day blows that cell, you'll have 60 seconds to hightail it out of there.

Maverick nodded his head in agreement, "Will do!"

Diplomat adjusted himself in his chair. A smaller screen appeared in the top part of the monitor. Numbers and a map appeared on the screen as Diplomat typed.

"Maverick, the Scrolls are four miles' deep underneath the mountain. Let me see. I'm getting the coordinates now. Got it! Three miles east of SD1."

Octane leaned forward in the seat. "Maverick, you know what will happen once we drop those explosives?"

Modern Day put the car into self-drive mode as he made a circle with both his hands.

Maverick nodded his head in agreement and made the same gesture. "Yes, yes. Exactly."

Diplomat continued to type, "I'm programming an illusion of the vehicles entering the mountain. When you get within five miles of the mountain, High Octane will appear to the outside guards as a supply truck. That's when you'll ..."

Octane nodded his head as he looked at the map. High Octane was also being tracked. The red dot was heading towards the blue glowing star.

"Yep, I got you, Diplomat. You must guide us from within, my friend."

"You can count on me." Diplomat responded. Modern Day and Octane headed towards the mountains. It was almost show time.

22

It was around six thirty in the evening when Maverick disconnected himself from the conference screen. He walked into his bedroom and began to put on his K.A.T.H.I.N.S. suit. He moved so slowly because his mind was somewhere else. It was on the mission.

"I trust Octane and I know he trusts me. I just hope Maria can trust us." Maverick said to himself as he walked to the top of his mansion to the heliport where Sky Guardian is located. He walked to the super machine and tapped it.

"Well, here we go again, my old pal." Maverick said to himself. He was alone and he had to psych himself up. He always did this when he had to go on a dangerous mission. However, this one was different than the others. One of their own was caught up and may be in the clutches of their mortal enemy. No one knew if she was still even alive. He didn't want to think that way. Besides, he would know anyway. He had that gift.

Maverick lifted his arm in the air and began to shout at the top of his lungs. "This is for The K.A.T.H.I.N.S. This is for Merciful. You'll pay, Amdogata. Mark my words!"

Maverick jumped into Sky Guardian. He
buckled up and pressed a few buttons before
starting the ignition. He heard the familiar noise
of the engines powering up. He prepared
himself for the force of the takeoff. Once the
engines were warmed up, Maverick turned on
the ignition to take off and he felt himself get
pushed back as Sky Guardian lifted from the
heliport and departed from the mansion at over
600 miles per hour.

By the time, he was in the air, he pushed
a few more buttons and put in the coordinates to
the San Fernando Valley. He was connected to
Merciful and he knew she was still alive. As
long as he didn't have any visions, he knew
everything was fine. He hit Mach 1 as he flew
to the valley. His mindset on completing the
mission. He then hesitated.

"I must set the exact coordinates, one
wrong move and the whole mission is over
before the right time and that could be
detrimental to the team.

Maverick continued to fly over Mount
Vernon, while trying to strategize over how he
would attack. He exceeded Mach 1 to ensure
that the Air Force wouldn't mistake him for an
airstrike. He sent a message to Diplomat to gain
flight clearance for him. Diplomat retrieved that

in five minutes. He was almost ready to go on his mission.

Maverick then turned Sky Guardian towards the Valley. He was only ten miles away from the target location and he knew he would get there before Octane and Modern Day. He knew he had to be there just as they arrived so that he could get Merciful to safety as quickly as possible. It would be one less thing for them to worry about. It would also throw Amdogata off their tracks and those of the Secret Scrolls.

He looked at his clock.

He had more than enough time.

He keyed in a few numbers. Maverick spoke to himself.

"Ready when you are."

23

Riding in silence, Octane and Modern Day were ten miles away from Gross's mountain headquarters. They rode through the mountains, in a place where there were no paths and only wildlife lived. They passed dozens of wolves and coyotes as they rode towards Merciful. Diplomat was still typing on the computer when Octane broke the tension in the air, "Diplomat, are you ready?"

"Yes, Octane I'm setting you up right now. In five, four, three, two, one."

High Octane was one of the most technologically advanced vehicles in the world and one of the best features of the car was its ability to shapeshift. In order to go undetected into Gross's secret lair, Diplomat typed in a few codes and High Octane was transformed into an equipment truck complete with the Gross logo on the side of the car. However, the disguise only lasts for 20 minutes.

"Now, don't think it's that easy." Diplomat continued, "I'm printing out two fake ID badges so you can get past the guards. They will be ready in three, two, one..."

Two IDs appeared at the bottom of the monitor.

"Just in time." Modern Day said, "Here comes the guards now, Darrel."

Octane grabbed both cards from the port. Modern Day slowed the car to a stop as they approached the gate. Octane handed Modern Day the cards. Modern Day rolled down the window and handed the guard on the left the two badges. The IDs were illuminated with a blue light as the Android guard scanned the IDs. He looked up and nodded his head. The gates opened. Octane raised his hand as they drove past.

"Hail Amdogata!"

It took everything for Modern Day to keep his face straight. He didn't want to show any anger. He knew it would blow their cover. He turned to Octane briefly to hide his disgust. The Android guard nodded again.

"Hail Amdogata." the Guard said. "Let them through."

Before they were able to make it towards the headquarters, they were stopped by another Android guard.

"Wait, what sector are you going to?"

Modern Day tried not to panic. "Sector C, my good man. Hail Amdogata."

The guard nodded his head. "Okay, you shall continue. Hail Amdogata."

Modern Day and Octane were finally free. They drove through the gates. The monitor came back on and Diplomat reappeared on the screen. "Close one, huh guys?"

"We're talking about close. We're going to have to definitely talk about that one."

"Where is Sector C?" Modern Day asked.

Diplomat typed on the computer. "Sector C is located on the east side of the building. That might be where they are also holding Merciful and SD1."

"Got it." Modern Day replied. Octane and Modern Day continued their drive towards Sector C.

"Maverick, are you ready to move into position?" Octane asked.

Maverick also appeared on the screen. "I'm right above you. I have locked in the exact coordinates for SD1. Alkaline is here for outside support."

The coordinates appeared on the screen. Maverick continued,

"Okay I've located the scrolls and SD1. I'm ready for the signal."

"I'll give you the word." Octane said.

"Got it." Maverick said. Maverick pressed a few buttons and Octane heard the jet engines above.

"Time for another mission."

After a few moments, Modern Day parked the vehicle. Octane jumped out to recover.

24

Merciful had blacked out after her confrontation with Todd and Amdogata. She didn't know how long she was there when she finally regained consciousness. All she remembered was screaming at Amdogata and then came the terrible headache. She wasn't one who always called for help, but she had to admit that she needed her team. With her helmet gone, she would be unable to communicate with any of them. She was also scared that Amdogata would get a hold of the others.

Merciful looked for her helmet. It should stick out since the room she was in was all white. Todd was in here earlier, but now he was nowhere to be found. "There may be some hope to this." She thought. She turned her head to the small table to the left and lo and behold, there was her helmet. It was glowing. They found her. She smiled as the red light in the middle of the helmet turned on. That means that she would be able to talk to the rest of the K.A.T.H.I.N.S.

She heard Diplomat's voice. It was faint, but she could make out what he was saying.

"Finally." Diplomat's voice said over the speaker. "Are you there? Merciful? Are you there?"

"Yes." She said, as loud as she could. She didn't want to alert anyone to what was going on.

"Modern Day, Octane and Maverick are here. What does your room look like? I have the coordinates to the building, but not to the exact room. Do you remember how you got there?"

"No, I don't." Merciful replied. "But I can tell you that the room is all white and that there is only one door. No windows. That's all I can say."

"Thank you, Merciful." Diplomat said, soothingly. "That was more than enough considering everything that happened today."

Merciful nodded her head while she tried to hold back tears. Diplomat continued,

"Modern Day and Octane are in the building but they are unable to find you, even with the helmet next to you. That means you may be underground or in some sort of concrete or metal building. They have on the suits so they may be able to lock you in once they get into a closer range. Maverick and I are watching them from above and from the headquarters. We got you."

Merciful managed to smile.

Modern Day and Octane found themselves following a few Androids through the abandoned tunnels. They brought in two boxes with them. They were full of weaponry they would use to save Merciful. Weapons such as electrical disrupters and explosives that were able to blow through titanium doors. Maverick had given Octane a rough layout of how the original Gross Industries headquarters were designed. So, they knew they would have to up the ante when dealing with the secret lair. They had to get to Merciful and the Scrolls before Amdogata did.

"Turn left." Octane said. "We need to separate from the group without others noticing. Once we clear that, we need to jump in that vent to the right."

Modern Day nodded his head. "Perfect. Those types of vents usually lead to basements. We can run through those and may be able to find Merciful."

"On my count." Octane said.

"Got you." Modern Day said.

They continued to walk, slowing down the pace until they were far behind the other Androids. Octane gave him the safety wink and they ran to the left. However, instead of finding vents they could cut through, they were greeted with three titanium doors.

"Wait for it." Octane said. He waited about three seconds before reaching into his box and pulled out two explosives. He pulled the pins and threw them at the door. They ran away from the hall and towards the exit. There was no Android to be found. The coast was clear. They called Maverick on the K.A.T.H.I.N.S. communicator.

"Maverick!" Octane yelled. "We are about to detonate the bomb. I think that Merciful is located behind one of those three doors. I want you to be in position to retrieve Merciful and take her back to the headquarters."

Maverick's voice was heard over the speaker. "Roger that."

"Okay, we are about to detonate." Octane took out his communicator and pressed a few buttons. Modern Day and Octane hit the ground as they felt the warmth and saw the flash of the grenades. Metal and rock flew everywhere. They had blown through the doors. Octane and Modern Day got back up and ran towards the hallway.

"It's done." Modern Day said into his communicator. "Let's go find our girl."

"You go get Merciful and I will find SD1.

Maverick nodded his head. "Got you."

Octane and Modern Day ran through the doors.

Maverick pushed a couple buttons and Sky Guardian instantly went into stealth mode. To remain undetected for as long as possible, Maverick swooped down near the mountains and did a quick surveillance of the area. He knew the familiar glow of the Secret Scrolls. They were so powerful that they couldn't be concealed unless they were buried deep within the earth. He didn't detect them. That means they were still digging for them. He didn't know how long it would take before Todd and his Androids reached them.

He then got back into formation and headed towards the all-white building that was located roughly a mile away from the mountain. Diplomat was right. This was definitely the place. A strange noise started to sound. It was a loud, whooping noise. He was detected.

Octane pressed a button on the side of his helmet. Appearing on the front of the screen was the location of SD1. It was in a room not too far from where he stood. He was alone. No sign of Todd or any Androids.

"This was too easy." He thought to himself as he walked past the third titanium door. And there she was, SD1, glowing blue, on a table. By itself. He ran into the room and removed the bike from the table. Just as he was about to pull it upright and ride the bike to safety, a strange alarm sound came on, followed by a hissing.

They had been discovered and the place was being destroyed. Octane was praying that Modern Day already located Merciful and was on the way out. Pressing on the speaker of his K.A.T.H.I.N.S. helmet, he called for Modern Day.

There was no answer.

He pressed the button again and waited for a few seconds.

Still no answer.

He trusted that everything was fine, but he knew he had to leave and make sure that everything was okay. He was the leader of the K.A.T.H.I.N.S. He had to make sure that everyone was safe. So, leaving SD1 there, Octane locked in his helmet with the location of Modern Day.

The sounds of the alarms startled Merciful. She began to panic. What did the sound mean? Would they find her in time?

All she could do was hope. There was a strange smell, a slightly citrusy smell that made her feel really drowsy. She had to stay awake. She heard a strange noise at the door. Her heart stopped, thinking it was Todd or one of the Androids. She prepared herself for the worse until she saw a familiar helmet, a K.A.T.H.I.N.S. helmet, peak around the corner. It was Modern Day. He ran up to her.

"Are you good?" He asked her.

"Now that you're here, yes. Is Octane here with you?"

"As always." Modern Day replied, winking at her. He reached behind his back and pulled out some chain cutters. With four quick snips, Merciful was free. She stretched her arms and legs.

"No time to waste. We have to go." Modern Day said. Merciful did her best to run over to the table and grabbed her helmet. She almost fell.

"I can't really run. My arms and legs feel so weak and I am so tired." Merciful leaned against the table.

"I'll just slow you down. Leave me here. It's okay."

Modern Day shook his head vigorously. "We never leave anyone behind. I got you."

With the alarms still sounding, Modern Day threw Merciful over his shoulder and headed to the door. They ran down the hallway. Merciful was so heavy. She had completely passed out from the gas that had been leaked into her room. Modern Day's helmet detected a chloroform-like substance in the air. Oxygen immediately started pumping into his mask. Thankfully, Merciful didn't inhale too much of it. She would recover just fine once she was safely at the headquarters. They found Octane.

"We have to get out of here now. They are on to us." Octane yelled. Modern Day looked to the left and saw four Androids run into the tunnel after them.

"There will be more." Octane continued.

The Androids all of a sudden stopped and raised their right arms, pointing them at the K.A.T.H.I.N.S.

Modern Day's eyes widened as their arms turned into guns. They were so close to the exit. All they had to do was run one hundred more feet or so and they were free. They would be safe.

"Oh shoot." Modern Day said as he saw red lasers being fired from their fingers. "Put on her helmet, Octane."

Octane ran behind Modern Day and put the helmet on Merciful's head. They then began to run towards the exit. Although, their suits would protect them from any harm, they dodged the laser bullets as they made their way towards the end of the tunnel. The lasers lit their path.

"Keep running towards the exit. Get Merciful to safety. Maverick will be waiting for you right outside." Octane yelled as he turned around and took out his favorite weapon. He pulled it out of the box and aimed it at the Androids. There must have been at least fifty of them, but he knew his trusty EMF scrambler would be able to take them all out, as well as any Android that was in a half-mile radius.

Octane dropped to his knees. Placing the EMF scrambler over his shoulder, he powered it up. As the Androids ran to him from all sides, the walls and crawling on the ceiling, Octane took aim and fired. The shockwaves made the walls moved, and the force knocked him about three feet back. He heard the sounds of banging metal as the Androids shut down and fell against each other, one by one, ten by ten until none were left standing. Octane stood up and made his way to the exit.

Octane heard a weird rumble as he finally reached the exit. He turned around as he saw rocks and boulders quickly fill up the manmade tunnel. He saw a weird blue glow as SD1 rode its way through the rubble. Maverick was waiting for them on the other side. Octane gave him the thumbs up as he ran to High Octane. He opened up the back doors and SD1 self-parked itself inside. Octane shut the doors and jumped into the driver's seat.

The disguise was gone.

As High Octane returned to its normal form, Octane turned on the ignition and kicked up the speed. He initiated K.A.T.H.I.N.S. mode which turbo-boosted the vehicle into high gear. If he wasn't careful, he could blast through the mountainside and right into Bel Air. The mountains were crumbling around them as well as the secret headquarters. They did not want to be trapped. High Octane had already reached 1,000 miles per hour before Maverick was able to navigate Sky Guardian directly above High Octane. Maverick appeared on the monitor.

"We have to link so you can get me out of here. Activate joining sequence." Octane said.

"Got it." Maverick replied. "I'm already above you. Let me know when I need to lower Sky Guardian."

The ground continued to shake as the mountains changed shape. Octane pressed a few buttons on the dashboard. "I'm ready." Octane said.

Maverick lowered Sky Guardian directly on top of High Octane. He felt the car bounce as the two machines connected and pulled High Octane high into the clouds. They flew over the

Pacific Ocean as flames shot and spun from the six exhaust pipes at the bottom of the vehicles. They were on their way to the K.A.T.H.I.N.S. headquarters.

25

They finally arrived at Mount Vernon.
The K.A.T.H.I.N.S. headquarters was waiting
for them, ready to repair any damages, both
physical and otherwise. Maverick landed High
Octane safely on the tarmac. He detached
himself and shortly after landed Sky Guardian
on the heliport about twenty feet away.
Maverick turned around. Merciful was leaning
on Modern Day's shoulder. She was starting to
regain consciousness.

Octane sat in the car for a few moments.
He felt like he failed the mission. Thank
goodness that he was able to save Merciful, but
he was unsure of what happened to the Secret
Scrolls. Who had them now? Did Amdogata get
his hands on them? Were they still in the
mountain? The only other thing that brought
him comfort about the Scrolls was that
Amdogata needed the other seven in order to
gain the true power they possessed. Once
Merciful was better, they would be able to
protect the other six and possibly retrieve the
seventh one from Amdogata. He put the faith
out there.

He took a few more deep breaths and
finally got out of High Octane. There was

minimal damage to both vehicles. He met up with Maverick and Modern Day who were helping Merciful out of Sky Guardian.

"Hey." Maverick said to Octane. "Are you looking for this?"

Octane recognized that familiar, otherworldly glow. It was the Scrolls. Maverick saved the Scrolls. At least, this set of the scrolls. Although the K.A.T.H.I.N.S. may have gained the upper hand on Amdogata this time; unfortunately, this is only one battle. The war was not over. There are still six more Secret Scrolls that needed to be protected. Octane knew that Amdogata would stop at nothing to retrieve them. At least, not until he is destroyed. It was only a matter of time before he would try again. But for now, Octane knew they could all rest. They were going to need it.

THE K.AT.H.I.N.S. BIOGRAPHY

Patrick Nolan Shackelford is a Deputy Probation Officer who loves to give back to the youth. He works with MPYD and other youth organizations to better the community. When Patrick was young, he had asthma and different groups like the YMCA helped him enjoy a close to normal life by giving him his inhaler while at the same time treating him like the rest of the kids.

Patrick attended to Cal State University Dominguez Hills, where he was given a part time opportunity with the Los Angeles School District under the YS Care Program to help at-risk youth create short movies and stories.